Bloody Reasons

Bloody Reasons

To Kill A Man, Book One

Stuart G. Yates

Also by Stuart G. Yates

- Unflinching
- In The Blood
- To Die in Glory
- Varangian
- Varangian 2 (King of the Norse)
- Burnt Offerings
- Whipped Up
- Splintered Ice
- The Sandman Cometh
- Roadkill
- Tears in the Fabric of Time
- Sallowed Blood
- Lament for Darley Dene
- The Pawnbroker

'The easiest way for a man to be killed is for word to get out that he backs down when somebody thinks he has the upper hand'
Attributed to Bat Masterson, famed gunfighter and lawman

'But Masterson always was full of... sheep-dip.'
Spoken by John Bernard Books in the film 'The Shootist'.

For the good friends I've known along the way and for Janice for showing me the right direction

1

"What the hell is this?"

The two men sat astride their horses – horses which refused to move any closer, despite their vain efforts, which included shouting, kicking and slapping. Frustrated, the two men gave up.

Across from them, no more than twenty paces away, stood the tiny taverna. A raven-headed whore stood outside. Her skirts were hitched up to reveal a well-muscled thigh, one booted foot propped on a small stool as she rubbed olive oil into her flesh. She threw back her hair and smiled in their direction.

"That is his woman," said the Mexican, kicking at his horse's flanks one last time. The animal still refused to budge.

"Damn it, if she ain't the prettiest damned thing I've seen in a month of Sundays," drooled the man beside the Mexican. He sucked at his teeth. "How old would you say she is?"

"I don't know, maybe forty. But if you try anything on with her, he'll kill you."

"He'll try."

"If he's inside, he'll kill you."

"Well, we'll just have to see about that, won't we?"

The man eased himself from the saddle and dropped to the ground. Hands on hips, he stretched his back, the long grey coat hanging open to reveal two revolvers at his belt, butts pointing inwards. He tried a wide-mouthed grin in her direction and she stood straight, hands on her own hips in a mocking imitation of him, pelvis thrusting provocatively forward. He cackled. "Shoot, she is flirting with me, Sanchez."

"She is playing you for a fool, Root."

"Nah. I think she likes what she sees."

Root rolled his shoulders and strolled nonchalantly towards her, taking his time, pulling out a tiny cotton bag from his right vest pocket. From the other, he produced a cigarette paper, trickled tobacco from the bag along it, drew the bag shut with his teeth and put it away. Running his tongue along the edge of the paper, he rolled it expertly and tightly and popped it into the corner of his mouth. Upon reaching the taverna, he stepped up onto the creaking, dilapidated veranda and stared directly into her smouldering, black eyes.

"My, you sure is pretty."

"*Gracias,*" she said.

"What's your name?"

"Maria."

"Yeah... of course it is."

She pulled out a long match from somewhere amongst the folds of her skirt and ran the head along the wall adjacent to the open door. It flared into life. Cupping the flame with her hands, she offered it to him, and Root obliged, leaning into her, lighting his cigarette. He inhaled deeply, the paper sizzling as the dry tobacco smouldered brightly. Releasing a long stream of smoke, he picked at his teeth with his free hand and nodded to the interior of the taverna. "I'm looking for a friend of mine. Last I heard, he was inside."

"My last customer is inside. He is young." She cast her eyes around, an impish light playing around her face. "He is young and *very* energetic."

"Is he, by God?"

Nodding, Maria looked away – feigning coyness, Root decided. Without warning, Root shot his right hand out to grab her crotch. She cried out and he slammed her against the wall, blew smoke in her face, then kissed her before she could cough.

When at last he pulled back, gasping, she pressed the back of her hand against her lips, saw the spots of blood on her skin and hissed, "Bastard." Screwing up her lovely face in fury, she launched a punch in his direction, but Root turned and parried the blow, grabbing her wrist with his right hand. He grinned as she desperately tried to break free.

Her efforts proved useless and Root squeezed. She cried out, "Let me go, you *gringo* sonofabitch!" She struggled against him, but her protestations merely resulted in him tightening his grip still further and she squealed, dropping to her knees, tears springing from her eyes. "*Please, señor…*"

A man stepped out from the gloom of the taverna and put a bullet through Root's head. In one easy, flowing movement, he altered his aim slightly and put another bullet into the throat of the Mexican as he struggled to turn his horse away. Hands flew to where the blood boiled, and Sanchez gurgled and screamed until the lights went out. His body fell to the dirt, where he lay, legs twitching now and then until he died. His terrified horse bolted, along with the second animal and, as the echoes of the gunshot dwindled away into the far-off mountains, the silence gradually settled once more.

The man with the gun got down to the girl's level and helped her to her feet. She sobbed into his chest as he drew her to him. He kissed her on the cheek and stared down at the dead man lying on his back, eyes wide open in total disbelief, the hole between his eyes a perfect circle, smoke still curling from the cigarette protruding from his thin, pale, dead lips.

"Wonder who they was?" said the young man, slipping his revolver back into its holster. He led Maria back inside, his hand already disappearing beneath her skirt to find her firm buttocks.

2

Gus Ritter leaned on the bar counter, idly turning the beer glass in his palms, lost in thought.

He'd ridden for three days straight, sleeping as best he could in the saddle, forced to stop and camp only once on the journey. More for his horse's sake rather than his own, he'd decided to rest up for a while, found a slit in a rocky outcrop and managed to grab a few fitful hours. The horse ate oats, gulped down water and seemed, in the morning at least, renewed. He did his best not to push the mare too hard. If it were to die out there, in the wide, open prairie, he'd be rich pickings for the buzzards within a day.

And now he was here. Archangel. He pondered why anyone would choose such a name. Wasn't it something to do with God, or religion, or some such hokum? He never could fathom those stories as his old mom had never forced him to attend Sunday School, owing to her being drunk most days, and especially on the Sabbath. He chuckled at the memory. Poor old Mom. She'd been kicked in the head by their mule whilst cussing the animal and thrashing it across the rump with a stick. She got paid her dues when it lashed out with its hooves and broke her skull. Ritter never shed a tear.

He was eleven years old.

Thoughts of church and Bible stories seemed apt at that moment, as the batwing doors burst open and a heavy-set man in a long brown robe of coarse cloth strode in, his face a mask of pure fury. A couple of

4

old men in the corner took one look and, cards and drinks forgotten, made a quick exit.

"Now, padre—" said the barkeep sharply. He quickly put down the glass he had been polishing and strode over to the swing hatch at the end of the counter.

"You hold your tongue, Wilbur," snapped the padre and moved to the far end, where a fat, slovenly-looking individual bent over the counter, spittle drooling from thick lips, a whisky tumbler before him, almost empty.

The padre stepped up to this miserable-looking individual and jabbed him in the arm with a thick finger. The man groaned, muttering some indecipherable garbage from his slack mouth, and peered at the padre with narrow, unblinking eyes. "Ah, shit, Father. What the hell are you—"

Moving fast for such a big man, the padre gripped the fat man by the shoulder and swung him around, slamming his knee upwards into the crotch. The man squawked, and the padre swung a looping left into the man's temple, smashing him against the edge of the counter. Crying out again, the man retched as if he were about to vomit before the padre sent him reeling backwards with a tremendous right punch straight into his nose.

Crashing against the far wall, the man slid to the floor, blood leaking from his face like beer from the barroom tap to mix with a stream of puke covering his shirt front. In a blur, the padre was on him as if possessed, raining down punches, the screams of the fat man drowned by the sound of smashing bones and the squelch of blood.

Ritter saw it, but didn't believe it. A man of God? A padre? He was certainly not like any country parson Ritter had ever laid eyes on. He sighed, returned to his beer and drained the glass.

"Padre, you needn't have done any of that," said the barkeep, moving across the barroom towards the blubbering fat man on the ground. "I try to keep a decent establishment and you've just about undone six months of good house-keeping right here with all of this bullshit." He got down on his haunches and studied the semi-conscious man's face.

"Dear God, you sure bust him up real good. What the hell is all this about?"

The padre, breathing hard, struggled to control the anger in his voice. "You tell that bastard when he wakes up, he has until sunup to get out of town. If he ain't gone by then, I'm gonna come a-calling."

"That still don't tell me what this is about."

"Wilbur, is you an old woman, or is you an old woman? Just do what I damn well say."

Shaking his head, Wilbur stood up, placing his hands on his hips. "He's got friends."

"If they are anything like him, then I'll kick their butts, too."

"I don't know what in hell has gone on here, padre, but something tells me it ain't gonna end well."

"He took the Parker girl into a barn and he had his way with her."

Gaping, Wilbur looked from the priest and back to the fat man. "Nati Parker?"

"No, her younger sister, Florence."

"Shit. She ain't but—"

"She's thirteen, Wilbur. This bastard violated her."

"Shit…"

"Her sister found her in a dreadful state. This bastard had beaten her, torn off her dress and had his way. I won't tolerate that, not from anyone. You understand me, Wilbur – I will not tolerate it. So, you tell this miserable piece of filth, if he ain't gone by tomorrow, I'll see he hangs."

And with that, the padre whirled around and stomped out of the bar.

Gus Ritter watched him go and whistled silently through pursed lips. "Damn, that man is hell on wheels."

"He sure is," said Wilbur, prodding the fat man with his boot. By now, he was fully unconscious. "I don't think I've ever seen him so riled."

"Ain't you got no sheriff to sort such troubles out?"

"No. Sheriff Herbert fell down and died not six or seven weeks ago from a failed heart. We ain't had the necessary to swear in a replacement yet. There's supposed to be a marshal coming down from Cheyenne to oversee it all, but we ain't heard nothin' from anyone. Nobody gives a good damn about Archangel, not even those of us who live here."

"You said he has friends."

"Yes…" Wilbur ruminated around in his empty mouth. "I can see trouble coming. There is old Silas, the uncle, his two boys, and a couple of firebrand working partners called Jessup and Martindale. They is trouble, mister. Been a-hootin' and a-hollerin' every Saturday night for weeks, shooting up bars, dance halls and the like. I had a set-to with 'em, fired my sawn-off and scared the shit out of 'em. They don't bother me no more. But this…" He shook his head again, gazing down at the fat man. "This here is Tobias Scrimshaw and his uncle, old Silas, owns a cattle ranch not more than ten miles from here. He has more money than sense, that old bastard, but he is meaner than a hornet with a toothache."

"I didn't know hornets had any teeth."

Wilbur gave him a look. "Mister, if you is fixing on buying another beer, then do it. If not, you take your clever remarks someplace else. I ain't in the mood."

Ritter shrugged and pushed the empty glass away. "I's about finished, anyway." He swung around and returned Wilbur's scowl. "And don't be thinking I'm like those two boys you scared with your sawn-off, *Mister* barkeep, 'cause I ain't. I don't take kindly to being spoken to like some rat in a barrel." He patted the Colt Cavalry at his hip. "My journey has been long and hard and it ain't finished yet. Aggravation, I can do without."

"Journey? What journey?" Wilbur frowned, eyes dropping to the revolver for the first time. "You wear that gun like you is capable of using it."

"Don't see no point in having a firearm if you can't use it."

"Yeah, but… Mister, what is your business here?"

"I'm lookin' for someone, is all."

"Someone important?"

"You could say." Ritter drew in a deep breath. "But he ain't here, and that has pissed me off some."

"Who is it you is looking for?"

"I wanted to ask you the same thing, but then the padre arrived and shot everything to pieces."

"Well, I might know. I tend to know everyone in this here town. If I don't, Cable Hughes over in the Wishing Bone saloon will know, but he rarely opens nowadays, thanks to those Jessup and Martindale bastards."

"Maybe you can help."

"Maybe I can." Wilbur tilted his head to one side. "For a price."

Ritter smiled, fished inside his waistcoat pocket and snapped a silver dollar on the counter top. "That should do it."

"Yes," said Wilbur, licking his lips. "A second might get you even more."

"Don't push it, barkeep."

Something changed in Wilbur's demeanour, his previous bravado swiftly replaced by a tremor of fear running across his lips. Perhaps he saw something he hadn't seen before, thought Ritter, and drew comfort from the fact. The barkeep gulped, his eyes flickering from the dollar to Ritter's Colt. "What's this person's name?"

"John Wesley Hardin."

3

The street brimmed with people going about their daily routines. Ritter doffed his hat to the occasional passing lady, nodded to various men, most of whom looked at him askance, frowning at his tieddown gun. Few held his stare. Ritter carried the air of a man confident in his own abilities – but just what these were, most citizens of Archangel that blustery morning preferred not to ponder on. Few of his sort passed through the town streets, but when they did, it invariably meant trouble.

He went into a small coffee-house and ordered a midday meal of eggs and bacon. Ignoring the stares of the other customers, he looked out of the window towards the many shops and service businesses lining the street. A group of shirt-sleeved men laboured like ants around a large, semi-completed building and he studied them with keen interest.

The waitress loomed over him and placed a full plate of food in front of him. He smiled. "Busy place."

"Yes," she said, following his gaze to the street. "And it'll be getting busier with any luck."

Grunting, he turned to his meal, enjoying every mouthful.

Later, having paid the bill, he crossed the street. Stopping beneath the swinging sign of The Wishbone Saloon, Ritter leaned forward to read the notice pinned to the boarded-up entrance. Lessons in Miss Winters' one-room school house back in Denver had given him a basic knowledge of words, but he continued to find difficulty with more complex sentences.

"It says we're closed due to the excessive libations of certain hot-headed individuals who caused inappropriate and extensive damage to this establishment."

Frowning, Ritter turned to regard the owner of the voice, a swarthy-looking individual with a cheery face and ample midriff. "You'd be Cable Hughes?"

The man tilted his head, arching a single eyebrow. "I am. I am the owner of this here establishment."

"So I understand." He gestured towards the sign. "These here 'hot-headed individuals', they be—"

"Two gunhands from the Scrimshaw ranch. Jessup and Martindale, I understand them to be called. A nastier pair I have yet to meet."

Ritter stepped up onto the boardwalk fronting the saloon and tapped the notice. "What is 'libations'?"

"Drinking."

"Ah... So they was drunk?"

"Beyond drunk, sir. Could I ask you what is your interest?"

"I am travelling through the State, looking for a certain fugitive from justice."

"An outlaw?"

"A killer."

Sucking in his breath, Hughes rocked back on his heels. "A killer? That sounds somewhat dramatic."

"It is."

Surveying Ritter from head to foot, Hughes' eyes settled on the other's revolver. "I'm surmising you are a bounty hunter?"

"What of it?"

Hughes held up his hands. "I am not judging you, sir, merely pointing out the obvious."

"My gun is my tool of trade. It enables me to make sense of a world which has lost its way. Violence, lawlessness, the abandonment of common decency... The War created deep divisions within us, Mr

Hughes, and it is all a man can do to find a path through it which does not lead him to confrontation and death."

"Yes, well, the War has been over these past eight or so years."

"Even so."

"Yes.... even so."

Ritter stepped down into the street again and stood level with Hughes, towering over the saloon owner by a good head. "You have plans on re-opening?"

"Perhaps. When those two trouble-makers have moved on."

"You think they will?"

"Who knows? Old man Scrimshaw has lost his way, leaving control of his business affairs to his sons." Hughes paused, glancing up and down the main street. A train of three wagons trundled by, pots and pans clanking against the sides. "More tenderfoots looking for the promise of a new life." He shook his head, forcing a smile at the lead driver as he moved on. "They sure as eggs is eggs won't find one here in Archangel."

"It seems prosperous enough."

"Oh, it is. When the railroad finally opens, it will be reborn. Merchant men, traders, shopkeepers, they are all making ready for that great day."

"Might even be the moment for you to re-open."

"Perhaps. Mister, who is it you are looking for? This so-called killer?"

"Nothing 'so-called' about it, Mr Hughes. I understood from my previous stopping place that he was headed this way."

"I know of no killers ever stopping by here."

"He doesn't advertise the fact. Indeed, if ever you set eyes upon him, you would find him a most respectable individual, well-dressed, polite, slight in stature. But if you looked close and caught the glint in his eyes, you'd see something you would not like. Unfortunately, such an action would almost certainly cause him to be affronted, or give him rise to suspect you were challenging him. No one has ever held his stare and lived."

"Dear God." His eyes widened as he latched on to something beyond Ritter's shoulder. "Blessed Jesus," he said, his face paling, "that looks like trouble."

Ritter swung around to see two horsemen charging up the main street. They dismounted at a run and charged towards the entrance to the saloon where Tobias Scrimshaw had received his beating. Ritter whistled as the riders burst through the batwing doors, their guns already materialising in their fists. "Yep, you could be right, Mr Hughes. They sure look like trouble to me."

"What in tarnation has gone on in there?"

"A beating," said Ritter. "Seems like your priest can dish it out with some considerable skill."

"You mean Father Merry?"

"I do indeed. Some fat man in there got the living shit kicked out of him, and now I suspect his friends have got wind of it."

"One of them looks like Reece, old Scrimshaw's youngest."

"They'll be wanting retribution from the priest."

"No doubt. Someone must have told Reece about what happened."

"There were two others there. Maybe it was one of them."

"People will stir up all sorts if they think they'll get paid for it."

Ritter nodded grimly. "I've a mind Father Merry may be the one I need to speak with about my quarry. The proprietor of yonder establishment told me as much, in exchange for a dollar. I do believe a man of the world such as the good padre would recognise John Wesley without so much as a blink."

"John Wesley...?"

Turning, Ritter saw the deathly pallor of the saloon owner and grinned. "Yeah, his name does tend to cause that reaction. Now, if you would be so kind, could you point me in Merry's direction?"

As Hughes opened his mouth to speak, the commotion across the street in the other bar came to a climax as the two men kicked through the doors, carrying the large, semi-conscious frame of Tobias between them. Behind them appeared the barkeep, wringing his hands, a troubled expression on his face which, when he caught sight of Ritter, turned to desperation. He gestured towards the bounty hunter and cut through the gathering groups of onlookers, all curious to see what was happening.

"They'll be meeting up with some others and going over to Father Merry's place, I shouldn't wonder," Hughes said, rattling off his words at a furious pace. "If I know them boys, they plan on killing him."

Grunting, Ritter swung around to face Hughes. "Well, seems I might have to skedaddle if I'm to make it to him first. Now, tell me where he lives."

4

Silas Scrimshaw rolled over onto his side and rattled out a long breath. "I'm not so sure I can do this for much longer."

Next to him, Manuela propped herself up on her elbow and gave him a searching look. Twenty-two years of age, half-Mexican, her skin as brown as a nut, she pursed her lips and smiled. "Silas, you be the finest man I have ever known."

Twisting his head to face her, he frowned. "Well, that's nice of you to say, my lovely, but I know that ain't so."

"Of course, it is." She reached out and brushed his cheek with the back of her forefinger. "You make me very happy."

Grunting, Silas threw back the covers and got out of bed. Blazing through the open window, the early morning sun flooded the room and he went across and gazed out at the wide, open plain. Closing his eyes, he pulled in a deep breath, allowing the rays to warm his body. "I wish I was thirty, even twenty years younger. Damn it to hell, Manuela," he swung around, eyes drinking her in, her body naked, supine on the bed, "where the hell have you been all my life?"

She giggled, seeming to relish his hungry expression, and allowed her hands to roam over her full breasts and across the flat of her belly. "For most of it, I was not even born."

"God, if you ain't the most beautiful thing I've ever seen in my life!"

Another giggle. She patted the empty space next to her. "Come and lie with me. Make me purr like a mountain lion again."

Silas made as if to speak, but was cut off by the sound of a rider galloping into the open yard in front of the sprawling ranch house. Swinging back to the window, he peered out and swore under his breath. "Ah shit, this looks like trouble."

Moving quickly to the bed, he pulled on his robe, tightened up the belt and strode out of the room, with Manuela's cry of, "Come back soon, my love," ringing in his ears.

Sweeping out into the landing, Silas leaned over the balustrade and peered down to the large, open entrance room of his beautiful home built in the Mexican style. Silas had always wanted to maximise the amount of light coming into the house and, right now, this helped him to clearly see the young cowboy striding forward, covered in dust and sweat, hat thrown back to dangle down his back by its chin cord, his hair a wild mess.

"What in the hell is going on, Reece? You look like you is fit to fall down in a stupor."

"Ah, hell, Pa," said Reece, "we got trouble."

Tugging his robe closer, fears confirmed, Silas padded along the landing and descended the stairs. "Where the hell is Grimes?"

"I don't know – I only just got here."

"Yeah, I saw you riding in." Reaching the bottom step, he paused, one hand on the rail. "What the hell is going on?"

"Tobias got himself beat up."

Silas squeezed his eyes shut. "Ah, damn. Is he in a bad way?"

"I don't know, I only heard it from some of the townsfolk." He looked about him. The room was dominated by a massive table, with seating enough for twenty people. Right now it was bare, the top scrubbed clean, ornate chairs neatly pushed under on all sides. Reece reached for the nearest, drew it back, flopped down and put his face in his hand. "He did something bad, Pa. Mighty bad."

Frowning, Silas went up to him and sat down to the young cowboy's right. "Tell me."

Dropping his hand, Reece hissed through his teeth, "He went and took the young Parker girl into a barn and ..." He shook his head. "He fucking raped her, Pa."

Silas gaped and for a moment didn't know what to say or think. He sat back, shoulders drooping, overcome by the enormity of his eldest son's words. "The youngest girl?"

"Uh-huh. Florence. She's thirteen years old, Pa."

"Oh, my God."

Silas's voice, low, tremulous, reflected Reece's mood and the two men sat in silence, staring into nothing for a long time.

A wiry man of indeterminant age waddled into the entrance room and pulled up short when he saw father and son. Seeming to sense the depressed atmosphere, he shuffled his feet and, clearing his throat, said, "Can I get you anything, sir?"

Without looking up, Silas nodded. "Bring me some of my old Scotch whisky, Grimes. I think we both need it."

As the old man went out, Reece turned to his father. "I came here as fast as I could. One or two of the boys are going to take Tobias to Doc Wilson's place. His nose is broken and I think he might be bleeding inside. He sure is bleeding everywhere else."

"Holy shit. I would never have thought old Harvey Parker could do such a thing."

"It wasn't Parker. Besides, he's dead."

"Hell, really? I didn't know. Who did it, then?"

"It was the priest – Father Merry."

Again, Silas's mouth fell open, struck dumb by the news.

"I've heard stories about that man," continued Reece. "He fought in the War, so I heard. Was a member of a group of marauders who ranged far and wide across the Shenandoah Valley. With the surrender, he, along with all that other scum, was given free pardon. Seems he found God..." he blew out his lips, scoffing, "but a murdering son of a bitch he will always be. And now he's shown his true colours, right enough."

"I find this all hard to believe, Reece. A *priest* kicked Toby's butt?"

"He might die, Pa."

"Well," Silas crossed his arms, "I don't give a good damn about that, Reece. Toby is just like his father – a fat, lazy turd."

"Pa, he is kin!"

"Kin or not, he's still a wastrel. Always has been. His mother begged me to take him in when Guthrie got himself killed. I suppose I felt duty-bound by family ties, but I have to admit I have never felt comfortable with it. And now, it seems my lack of good judgement in this matter has come home to bite me on the ass."

Reece pushed back his chair, glaring down at his father. "I never would have took you for a shirker, Pa."

"A *what*? Maybe you haven't heard your own words, boy – that waste of space has violated a young girl. Holy God damn, Reece, I will not support him in any of this, if that is what you is hoping."

"I just thought you might have at least gone to pay that bastard padre a visit, to let him know he can't do such things as beat up one of our own. We have a reputation to maintain, Pa."

"Well, that'll be as good as a pail of dog-shit if we go condoning what Tobias has done. No, best leave it well alone. I'll go speak to the priest when this has all blown over."

"That'll be too late."

"Don't you go confronting me on this, boy. My decision is final. I want nothing to do with rapists – be they kin or not. I'm better than that."

"*Rapists...* Dear God, do you hear yourself? As if you haven't done anything like it yourself."

Springing to his feet, before Reece could even raise an arm Silas struck his son a back-hander across the face, sending him crashing to the floor. Wheezing loudly, Silas leaned forward on the table, pressing his knuckles hard into the woodwork. He glared at his stricken son, who rolled over and sat up, dabbing at his bloodied mouth with the back of his hand. "I may have done some bad things in my time, boy, but rape was never one of them. I will not be associated with it and if Tobias is bleeding to death, then good riddance, I say."

Squinting at his blood-smeared hand, Reece climbed groggily to his feet. "That does it, Pa. I've suffered your indifference, your insults and bitterness for too long. I'll not suffer your abuse."

"Grow up, Reece. You insulted me, and if you think I would allow anyone to—"

"*Anyone*? Jesus, you sanctimonious old bastard – I'm your fucking son!"

"What're you fixing on doing, Reece? Riding out of here with your tail between your legs, to set up on your own?"

"I think it's about time I did. You never had any intention of leaving this ranch to me, anyways."

"No, that's right. I'm leaving it to Manuela."

The sound of the girl's name struck Reece harder than the back-handed slap he'd only moments ago received. He blinked repeatedly, his breathing shaky. "Dear God, she truly has possessed you, like the devil she is."

"I love her, you impudent whelp." He stood up straight as Grimes returned, holding a silver tray on which stood a cut-glass decanter and two matching tumblers. Silas released a long breath. "Pour out two good measures, Grimes. The boy here will be leaving shortly, but he can take a drink first."

"I'll not drink with you," spat Reece.

"Call it a good luck toast, Reece." He licked his lips as Grimes dutifully filled up the tumblers with two good measures of the golden liquid. Silas took one proffered glass and breathed in the whisky aroma before swallowing down a large mouthful.

Without a word, Reece took the second glass and drained it in one. "You're all heart, Pa."

"Just go, Reece. It's been a long time coming." He took another sip and narrowed his eyes towards his son. "But I warn you, boy – you go looking for that priest, to avenge what he did to your cousin, I'll put you in the ground myself."

"You're a bastard," said Reece. "I'm glad Ma didn't live to see you for what you have become – an unfeeling, uncaring old fart."

"Get out."

"And don't be worrying about me doing anything to that shit-faced priest – Jessup's already tooled up and looking for him."

Lowering his head, Silas sighed. "I just knew it, as soon as the words were out of your mouth about what happened. That stupid firebrand will get us all hung."

"There was a time when you wouldn't have given a good damn about the law – because *you was the law*! Now, you ain't nothing but a hen-pecked old retard for that lithesome young thing upstairs in your bed. She's addled your brains, Pa, and I'll not stay here and see any more of it."

"So you said. Now, is you as good as your word or not?"

Reece threw down his glass. It rolled across the table top and Grimes caught it before it fell and shattered into pieces of the floor. "Mario will hear of this."

"Mario hasn't got shit for brains, unlike you. He'll do what I tell him."

"Well, there's another good reason for me to go." He turned on his heels and strode away without a backward glance.

"Pour me another," said Silas, thrusting out his hand towards Grimes, who took the glass and did as he was bid. Watching the whisky trickle into the tumbler, Silas considered his son's words, but paid them little heed. Manuela was the best thing that had ever happened to him and, when he sat back down and heard her soft, bare-footed approach… felt her fingers kneading his shoulders, her warm lips nuzzling at his ear, he knew he couldn't give a fig for anyone else in the entire world.

5

With the heart-breaking sobs of the young girl ringing in his ears, Father Merry came out of the tiny bedroom and went to the hand pump. He worked the lever, splashing water over his hands, then his face. Temporally blinded, he groped around for a towel. A pair of soft hands pressed a coarse cloth into his grip and he grunted his thanks. Patting his face dry, he turned to Nati Parker standing before him.

A slender woman of just over thirty, Nati possessed the smouldering good looks which betrayed her Mexican heritage – dark eyes and raven-black hair pulled back from her smooth, burnished face. She ran her tongue over her teeth and said, "How is she?"

"A little better. It's going to take time, Nati."

"We both have plenty of that."

"Maybe not."

She titled her head. "What do you mean?"

"I beat the bastard who did this half to death. I may even have actually killed him."

His words brought no change to her blank expression. "A pity you didn't. That son of a whore deserves to be in the ground for what he did."

"Yes, but even so… His friends will come-a-calling, and when they find I'm not at home, they'll come here."

"Then I shall kill them."

"No. You do that, they'll hang you."

"Pah, what a horse-shit world it is that allows my sister to be raped by that bastard, and does not give me the chance to avenge what he did. What kind of law is that, eh, padre?"

"The thing is, they *are* the law round these parts, Nati."

"Then where is the justice?"

"There isn't any."

"Then I will find my own." She swung around and strode over to the door, above which hung a Spencer carbine. She took it down and worked through the loading mechanism with obvious skill. Grunting, she looked again at the priest. "When they come, I will shoot them. My father taught me how to use this when I was twelve. I do not think he ever believed that one day I would have to use it."

"There is another way." Merry stepped up to the rough-hewn table and sat down. She followed him, placing the carbine between them. Leaning across the table, he took her hands in his. "You could load up your wagon and make it across the trail to Oregon. Start again."

"What? You think it is so easy to simply start a new life? And what with? What would we do? Whoring?"

"Don't be so stupid. You could—"

"What else is there for women such as we to do, eh?" She threw herself back in her chair. "None of this was our fault – *none of it!*"

"I know that, but you cannot—"

"My father brought us here nearly twenty years ago. This is our home, padre. I have no husband, no man. Father died a year ago, six months after the fever took my mother. He died of a broken heart, crying every night until..." She bit down on her bottom lips, brushing away the tear that tumbled from her eye. "Have you any idea how hard life has been since then? No, of course you haven't. You sit in your church, dispensing your prayers and your absolutions, but you have no sense of the hardships ordinary people face. But face it we have, and face it we will. My father built this place with his own two hands, padre. He broke every bone, pulled every muscle and he did it *for us*. And now you tell me to turn away and run? From sons of whores who destroyed my sister's life? She is probably with child, padre. Think on that the next time you come up with one of your ridiculous solutions."

She crossed her arms and sat there, seething, her breaths coming in short, sharp snatches. Merry waited, not daring to catch her eyes, to see the anger there, the indignation, the strength of conviction.

Eventually, he blew out a long breath. "All right, Nati, I'm sorry. You're right, of course. To run away is not an option."

"What then? Fight them?"

"They'll kill you, after having had their way with you. And Florence."

Sucking in her bottom lip, she nodded towards the Spencer. "I have maybe seven bullets. How many will come? Six, eight, ten?" She gave a short, scoffing laugh. "I will save the last two for myself and Florence. Better to die than to suffer more indignity at their filthy hands."

"I agree."

She frowned at him. "You do? So, you think it is all right for them to assault us here, to do what they want, to cause the deaths of us both?"

"No, I don't think anything of the sort." He leaned back and delved into the folds of his rough brown robe and produced a Colt Navy revolver, conversion model. He hefted it in his hand. "I will stand with you."

She stared, wide-eyed. "What are you doing with a gun, padre?"

He shrugged. "Old habits. This little beauty got me out of some scrapes back in the War, so I think she can do so again. I practise most days and can still plug a nickel at twenty paces."

"The War? But... Padre, I do not understand. You're a man of God."

"I wasn't back then, Nati. Back then I was part of a troop of raiders. We did some unspeakable things, none of which I am proud of. When the War ended, I came back to Missouri, found my old ma and she sat me down and heard my confession."

She gaped at him. "Your own mother? But... You told her what you did?"

"Her father – my grandfather – was a priest, you see. I suppose she took it upon herself to continue the tradition." He smiled, looking back through the years to his younger self, kneeling before his mother, her hand upon his head, blessing him. "I took holy orders a year or so after that. I've never looked back."

"Until now."

"Some things test you, Nati. Today tested me worse than anything since General Lee signed the surrender. I thought I'd buried the man I was back there in Arlington, but I was wrong. I'm still the same murdering scoundrel I always was. I beat the living hell out of that man, Nati. It all came back – the hate. I don't think it's ever gone away."

6

They stopped within sight of the Scrimshaw ranch. Reece cast a glance towards Tobias, who was slumped over the neck of his horse, a constant moan escaping from his broken mouth. "Will you shut the hell up, you whining cloth head."

His companion, rangy and red-headed, cackled through blackened teeth. "Hell, he sounds like a fart trapped in a bottle."

"And you would do well to keep your mouth shut also, Kelly."

Kelly went to speak, but clearly thought better of it as Reece continued to snarl and glare.

Turning back to the view of the ranch, Reece let out a long sigh. "I was hoping Mario could talk some sense into Pa. The old bat has lost his sand."

"Mario knows about all of this?"

"I told him after Pa threw me out. Anyways, we don't need him, but I reckon it is prudent to wait and see. We'll have enough trouble going up against the priest without putting Pa in the mix."

"Trouble against a priest?" said Kelly, scoffing. He leaned over to his right, hawked and spat into the dirt. "Hell, he's nothing but a boil on my ass. I'll kill him myself if you wanna."

Turning towards his companion, Reece gave a shake of his head. "You obviously know nothing about Father Patrick Merry, or you wouldn't be spouting such verbal diarrhoea, Kelly."

"Well, I knows he wears a dress and spends all of his time talking in that rickety church of his. Ain't nothing about any of that to cause me troubles, Reece. You hired me as a gunhand, not to sit back and whistle *Dixie.*"

Sighing, Reece turned away. "First things first, we take Tobias here to get patched up."

"Doc Wilson was out on his rounds. Some lady is giving birth and he—"

"I couldn't give a good damn about what Doc Wilson is doing. I know an old woman down aways who used to be a nurse."

"We could try Wilson again. If Toby lasts that long." He looked at his companion and shook his head.

"Doc Wilson will have had news of what has happened by now and he'll send a telegraph to the US Marshal's office in Cheyenne as soon as Toby is at his door. We don't need that sort of aggravation. A Marshal is supposed to be coming here, anyways and I don't need any further complications. Besides, old Ma Donnington don't even know such things as telegraph wires exist. She still thinks Andrew Jackson is President."

"Who?"

Shaking his head in despair, Reece turned his gaze towards the ranch house. "We'll wait, and if Mario don't show up in another hour, we'll head off to Ma Donnington's and then pick up Martindale. Three of us should be enough to take care of the priest."

"If you say so."

"I do." He nodded towards a clump of sagebrush. "Tie up the horses over there. We may as well stretch ourselves out whilst we're waiting." He looked to the sky. "We have plenty of hours of daylight left. If the rain keeps off, we'll be well set to have this grisly mess sorted before sundown."

Grunting, Kelly led the horses to the bush as Reece jumped down from his mount and stretched out his back. "Damn your hide, Pa, you obstinate old coot," he mumbled and looked around for a place to lay himself down and get some rest before Mario deigned to arrive.

* * *

Kelly Jessup looped the reins around one of the more substantial branches and looked over his shoulder towards Reece, only to see him stretched out in the dirt, hat tipped over his eyes. Running his tongue over his bottom lip, Kelly ran through his options. It would stand him in good stead to put the priest in the ground, especially in Mario's eyes. Mario was a man he respected; one he could do business with, whose assertiveness and strength made him a range boss to be obeyed. Reece, on the other hand, was a hothead and not much else; a man full of bluster who talked a good fight but had neither the mettle nor the skills to see one through to the end. His reaction over Jessup's suggestion of taking out Father Merry revealed the depth of his gutless, spineless approach to life. A priest – a man of God – was not someone to be fearful of, he reasoned.

A loud grunt brought Jessup out of his reverie and he looked over to see Reece, now clearly asleep, rolling over onto his side. Jessup waited, holding his breath, the plan already formulating in his mind. If he rode across to the church right now, he could end all of this before it had even begun. Mario would reward him handsomely and everyone could get back to living their lives and doing what they did best – having a good time, drinking, gambling and making money. So, as quietly as he could, he tugged his horse free and led it away from the small encampment.

Every other step, he paused to look back to check Reece was still asleep. By now, Jessup's range boss was snoring loudly and poor old Tobias lay flat out. He grinned and, once he was well out of earshot, he climbed into the saddle and spurred his horse into a gentle canter.

Soon he would be at the church and this Father Merry character would get what was due.

7

Father Merry's neat yet tiny church lay a few miles out of town and Ritter approached it at a steady trot. White-washed walls, windows down each long side and a small belfry topped with red-tiles, gave the building a tranquil air and Ritter understood why the townsfolk would look forward to filling up the pews every Sunday morning. Both Wilbur the barkeep and Cable Hughes had asserted that Merry's sermons were eagerly anticipated and his flock was growing. People sought solace after the uncertainties of the War. Even now, with the hostilities long over, there were many who feared what they saw as a godless land. Men like Jesse James and John Wesley seemed to underline these sentiments, despite so many believing these killers to be champions of the downtrodden. Fear walked alongside every man, woman and child and Merry provided hope for a better world.

Salvation.

Ritter rubbed his chin. He had never believed in such things, but right now, sitting astride his horse, he could certainly sense something beyond the visible. Perhaps it was God.

He tied up his horse and clumped up the wooden steps to the door in his heavy boots. At the top, he paused to turn and survey the open prairie, the trail leading to the town of Archangel cutting a silver line through the coarse grass. If the men Wilbur told him about were to come seeking their vengeance, this would be the way they'd arrive. At least he would have ample warning.

Sighing, he turned to the church entrance, pushed down the handle and eased the door open.

The smell of new-mown hay, tinged slightly around the edges with cigar and pipe tobacco, greeted him as he stepped inside. Despite the low ceiling, his steps echoed around the small interior as he strode down a central aisle bedecked with beautifully maintained floorboards.

Towards the rear, and to the right, stood a pulpit, reached by a set of steps. Fashioned from oak, the ornately carved panelling was not something Ritter had expected to see in a small rural church. Frowning, he stepped closer and ran his fingers over the intricate latticework, impressed.

A movement over to his left caused him to swing around in a half crouch, right hand sweeping up the Colt Cavalry revolver from its holster, hammer already engaged, the entire movement fluid, without hesitation.

He gaped.

In the vestibule doorway, a woman stood, her face ashen with fear but her lips full and her eyes glowing. Her hands came up in supplication. "Don't shoot, stranger."

Easing down the hammer, Ritter straightened, studying the woman intently. From the way she bore herself, her black, pleated dress, the hair tucked under a bonnet, he guessed her to be no more than forty. Her unblemished skin shimmered as the colour slowly returned to her cheeks.

Sliding the gun into its holster, Ritter tried a smile. It was not returned. "Sorry, ma'am, you took me by surprise. I wasn't expecting anyone to be at home, except for the priest."

She frowned as she lowered her hands, the tension leaving her shoulders. "Father Merry? He's not here."

"Ah." Ritter cast his gaze back towards the church. "When do you think he'll return?"

"I couldn't say."

He watched her as she glided past him. Pausing before the congregation pews, she gave him a piercing stare. "What would such a man as you want with Father Merry?"

"Just a little information."

She gave a dismissive grunt. "Well, as far as I know he went visiting the Parker girls." Another searching look. "You're not from around these parts."

"No, ma'am, I ain't. You could say I'm just passing through."

She sniffed loudly. "You carry the smell of the prairie with you, mister. You could do with a bath."

Ritter chuckled and touched the brim of his hat, "I daresay I could. But I ain't got no time for such luxuries… Unless, of course, you is offering, that is." He grinned as her face took on a look of disgusted outrage and shock. "I jest, ma'am."

Averting her eyes, cheeks reddening, she absently smoothed down the front of her dress with perhaps a little more vigour than was necessary. "I'm glad to hear it." She continued on her way down the aisle. "I have done with my chores here, mister. I'll be on my way." She stopped at the main entrance. "I have to lock up."

"I didn't think churches were locked up." He took another look around. "Can't say I see much in here worth stealing. What's in the back?"

"Nothing that need concern you."

"I guess not." He approached the woman and stopped next to her, looking down at her slight frame. "You dress in black – is that because you is a widow?"

Her jawline coloured slightly. "I am, as it happens. My husband was lost to scrofula, if you must know."

"Sorry to hear that, ma'am. We are all of us blighted by disease nowadays." He saw her frown. "I lost my wife some half a dozen years ago. The young 'uns, too."

"How dreadful."

"Yes, it was."

An awkward silence followed, both of them lost in a dark moment as the memories loomed large.

At last, the woman took in a breath. "I'm sorry if I sounded harsh before, but you surprised me and I—"

Ritter held up a hand. "Ma'am, it is I who should apologise. I had no way of knowing there would be anyone inside, saving the priest, of course."

"Yes, you said you wanted to speak with him. There was some terrible mischief concerning somebody from the Scrimshaw ranch. Father Merry flew into a rage after Suzanne Carrow came in to tell him. Why she chose to burden Father Merry with such dreadful news I cannot say, but she did, and Father Merry became like something possessed, ranting and raving like he was—"

"I have heard the story, ma'am. I was in the saloon in town when Father Merry burst in and beat up some wastrel lounging in there."

"Oh my!"

"Yes, ma'am. It was not a thing for a lady such as yourself to witness. This Mrs Carrow, she—"

"She is not married. Never has been. She's a whore."

Ritter blinked. "Oh. You mean Father Merry, he—"

"Father Merry spends much of his time with the fallen, mister. He does the Lord's service in trying to turn such people away from the path of sin and corruption."

"Indeed, ma'am. Does he succeed?"

"He tries. But their weight of sin is deep and heavy."

Nodding, Ritter sighed. "Well, I guess he administers what and when he can. So," he slapped his thigh, "I must ride across and find him. The Parker's place, you said. In which direction might that—"

He froze.

The sound of an approaching horse brought their conversation to a sudden halt. The woman went to speak, but Ritter swiftly put a finger to her lips. "Quiet now," he whispered, "I want you to get yourself in that back room. Can it be locked?" She nodded, her eyes widening with alarm. "Then do it. And do not come out until you hear me call – do you understand?" Another nod. "Good. Now scoot."

Without a word, she gathered up the hem of her dress and rushed back down the aisle towards the vestibule. At the door, she shot him a glance and he snapped his head forward, urging her to get inside. She did so and Ritter took a moment to check his Colt. Then he carefully pressed his face up against the main church doors and peered out through the crack between them.

The solitary rider was a rangy-looking fellow, hat slung back off his face to reveal a wild mop of red hair. Reining in his horse, he waited, scanning all around him. Scratching his chin, his gaze rested on Ritter's horse. He seemed to reach a decision after a moment's thought, swivelled in his saddle and drew out a Winchester Model 1866 from its scabbard that was held at his own horse's flank. He jumped down, took another long look around the outside of the church, worked the lever of the rifle, and inched forward.

Tearing open the doors, Ritter sprang outside, the Colt Cavalry pointing unerringly towards the redhead, who stopped in mid-step, gaping.

Recovering somewhat after a few seconds, the redhead squawked, "Now, just who the hell might you be?"

"I could ask you the same question," said Ritter, eying the Winchester. "You don't look like you've come here for salvation."

"Oh, but I have. I'm here to see the padre, and I don't much like you aiming that cannon in my direction."

"Put the rifle down, boy, and tell me what your business is with Father Merry."

"I'm of a mind to say 'no' to you, mister, until you do likewise with that cannon. It's making me nervous."

"Drop your rifle and state your business."

"I ain't stating anything, mister. Not with that thing in my face."

"I'm not going to ask you again."

The redhead shifted his gaze slightly, as if something had caught his attention. He shrugged, bent his knees and dropped the rifle to the ground, then straightened up again with both hands raised. "There we are. I'm a good little boy when asked to do anything in a nice, polite tone."

Ritter grunting and eased off the hammer to his Colt.

Something struck him across the back of his head, something hard and heavy, projecting him over the church steps to the ground, which he hit with a solid thud. Dust invaded his mouth and nostrils, causing him to cough and splutter, but the searing pain across his skull caused all other thoughts to scurry away into the distant corners of his consciousness. A pair of faded boots came into his line of vision, followed by the sound of cackling laughter. He would have liked to have raised his revolver, as well as his head, but both ideas were far too difficult and he slipped away into all-consuming blackness.

8

"My, oh my," laughed Kelly Jessup, getting down on his haunches to prod the prone, unconscious stranger before him, "this here is not a very nice fella." He glanced up at the woman in the black dress standing before him, a heavy-handled spade in her hands. "Thank you kindly, ma'am. He would almost certainly have killed me."

"I knew him for a killer the moment he came into the church."

Jessup stood up. "Did you now?"

"Yes, I did. I've seen his like before, with his tied-down gun and that evil glint in his eyes. I lived in Dodge for a while, when my husband worked as a deputy there. The amount of times I witnessed men such as him filling up the jailhouse is beyond counting."

"Well, I'm glad for it, ma'am. He drew down on me before I could take a breath. I was only coming here to talk to the good padre, inform him of what has happened to Tobias."

"Tobias?"

"Yes, ma'am. Tobias Scrimshaw. I do believe this here scoundrel," he put his boot into the side of the stranger, who did not stir, "beat poor old Tobias half to death. The good padre was tending to a young girl whom this one here," another kick, "had tried to interfere with."

"Good Lord."

"I know. It hardly beggars belief." A third kick caused a slight moan to spill from the stranger's lips.

"I thought he might be dead."

Jessup shrugged and gave a loud guffaw. "No, ma'am, I'm afraid not. Sleeping, is all." He tilted his head. "You know him?"

"Never set eyes on him before."

"But you have me." She nodded and he did too. "Yeah, now I come to think of it... ain't you one of Ma Brimley's troupe?"

"I used to be."

"Ah." He chuckled. "Got converted, eh? I heard the padre was doing the Lord's good work over at Brimley's whorehouse, helping the ladies find God. I also heard it said it's not so much converting as what interests him, but *cavorting*." He threw his head back and laughed. Screeching in fury, the woman swung the spade. But Jessup moved swifter than a rattler, ducked under the full swing, slammed his fist into her midriff and left-hooked her across the jaw, dumping her ignominiously to the ground, where she lay totally still, a trail of blood trickling from her mouth.

"Damned fucking whores," he said, dusting off his sleeves for something to do. Rolling his shoulders, he blew out a breath before retreating a few steps to retrieve his Winchester. He blew the dust away from the firing mechanism and, taking the steps in one bound, strode into the church. He raised his voice. "Hey, padre, you in here?" Before striding to the vestibule door, he paused and listened. Satisfied no one was about, he put his foot through the door and blasted his way inside.

Working quickly, Jessup went through a glass-fronted cabinet to his right, pulling the doors open so violently, he almost tore them from their hinges. He swept away a pair of copper goblets and a silver tray and when his hand curled around a cut-glass decanter half-filled with ruby red wine, he stepped back, raised the open mouth to his lips and drank.

Gasping, he dragged the back of his hand across his mouth and went over to a small desk. He pulled open drawers, hurled away papers and empty envelopes and leaned forward on his hands to gaze into the distance.

After a few moments, he took another drink from the decanter and hurled it into the corner, the glass shattering against the wall. He paused in front of a framed painting of Jesus on the opposite wall and grinned. "Well, well, my good Lordy, where has that little priest of yours gone to, eh?"

He was starting to move away when he caught sight of the small, black-bound notebook lying on the floor. Having tossed it aside without thinking, he now paused to consider its significance, if indeed it had any. Kneeling, he opened it and sifted through the pages.

Names, scrawled in a spidery hand, gazed out at him. Each page devoted to individual persons, all of them women. Jessup's reading ability was rudimentary at best, but even he could recognise names such as Suzanne, Patricia, Eliza and, on the fourth turning of the pages, Natalia. He paused, sucking in his bottom lip. "Natalia," he said softly. "Or… Nati. Nati Parker. Well, well."

He stood up and bowed flamboyantly towards the painting. "Thank ye kindly, good Lordy. Seems like you've answered my prayers." He looked again at the page and read aloud in stuttering, awkward tones, "Par-ker ho-ome st-ead." He chuckled. "Well, well, my Lordy Jesus. I think that fine little lady a-lying out in the dust with her swollen jaw is going to have to tell me just where this here homestead is." He winked at the painting and went outside, Winchester and book in hand.

Continuing to laugh to himself at the success of his detective work, he stepped out into the sunlight and squinted across the ground to where the woman lay.

She lay alone.

"I'm here."

Jessup swung around, book dropping, Winchester coming up.

But too late.

Way too late.

The stranger's Colt Cavalry barked in his hand, sending two slugs slamming into Jessup's chest, hurling back into the church to smash against the nearest pew.

He lay there, dazed, confused, whimpering as his heartbeat pulsed through the two large holes in his chest, pumping out the blood, spilling it down his shirtfront.

A shape loomed up in front of him.

"Who do you work for, boy?"

"Oh…" managed Jessup, "you'll have to guess, you bastard."

The stranger's gun came up and flashed once more.

9

Wincing, Ritter went to pull his head away, but her fingers gripped him around the chin and forced him to face her once more. "Keep your head still, mister."

Ritter screwed up his eyes. "It hurts like sin, ma'am. Why the hell did you hit me?"

"I thought you was a killer. Seems I misjudged you."

She applied the damp cloth to Ritter's head again, then dipped it back into the pail of water beside her. Wringing out the material, she took to dabbing away at the vicious looking wound across Ritter's scalp.

"Are you feeling all right?"

He grunted. "I feel a little sick in the stomach."

"And your vision?"

"It was all right, until you sat me down here and made me go through this purgatory."

"It needs cleaning. My husband told me he'd seen men die in the war from the smallest of gunshot wounds. They became infected, so he said. He followed the writings of some British woman over in Russia who tended to the sick and believed cleanliness was the secret to preventing infection." She applied the cloth again and Ritter hissed. "Oh hush, you ain't nothing but a big baby."

Deciding to endure the rest of the cleansing in grim silence, Ritter sat on a rickety stool and stared at his boots, watching pink dribbles run from between the woman's fingers to splash on the open ground between them. After shooting the redheaded youth, Ritter had attempted to put his gun back in his holster, missed, stumbled and fallen. It had taken most of her strength to lift him up again.

At last, she finished and stepped away to study him. "I'm going to fashion some bandages from the altar cloth. Then you'll need to rest."

He looked up at her and frowned. "You don't look so good yourself, ma'am."

Instinctively, her hand came up to brush across the swelling under her eye. "He hit me real good, that rangy bustard."

"I never could stomach a man who could hit a woman. It's the sign of a coward, in my estimation."

"Well, I cannot say I'm unhappy that you killed him. I have an inkling he is part of the Scrimshaw bunch, and none of those vermin receive any sort of forgiveness from anyone I know."

"You know the Scrimshaw bunch?"

"Some of them. To my shame."

"I don't understand."

"Let me cut you a bandage then I'll explain. I think that's the least you deserve, after me landing such a heartless, unintentional blow upon your skull."

He couldn't help but laugh at the idea of a fully-weighted swing of a shovel being termed 'unintentional', but again he remained quiet.

He sat on the stool before the steps of the church, in full view of anyone who might be watching. A Henry rifle in the hands of a sharp-shooter lying amongst the non-too-distant hills over to his right could take him out before he even realised. He shifted uncomfortably on his seat and glanced across to the redhead's corpse and wondered again who he was. If he was one of Scrimshaw's boys and had, as Ritter assumed, come looking to seek retribution for what the priest had done, why had he come alone?

"I found some brandy in the vestibule," she said, coming down the steps with a small bottle in one hand and a white table-cloth in the other. "It might sting some."

It did and Ritter suppressed a cry as the alcohol hit the open wound across the back of his head. To ease his discomfort somewhat, she handed him the bottle and he drained it, smacked his lips and grinned. "You make a damned fine nurse, ma'am."

"I'm a whore, mister. That's what I am."

Ritter gasped and watched her ripping the cloth into long, narrow strips. Grunting from her exertions, she slowly bandaged up his head. "My husband and I decided to travel out west, to make something of our lives, but he succumbed to scrofula and I was forced to do what I had to do in order to survive. I was employed, if you could call it such, at Madame Brimley's bordello over on main street in Archangel."

"Pardon me saying so, but you don't look like a whore."

"Ah, and you'd know, I suppose."

"Well..." he shifted in his seat, "I have had some, er, dealings, as you might say."

"Father Merry took me out of that Godforsaken place. He paid old Ma Brimley a fair price, I have to say."

"He *bought* you?"

"Old Ma Brimley had invested heavily in me, given me food and lodgings. I had barely begun on my lying-down business when Father Merry took me in."

"I still don't get it. Why would an old preacher do any such—"

"There's a lot you don't know, mister, and I ain't gonna fill in the gaps for you, but I'll tell you this – Father Merry ain't old. He is as fit as any young buck I've ever..."

Her voice trailed away, her eyes growing wet. She sniffed loudly. "I think they plan on killing him. Why else send such a pierce of slime as him," she jerked her head towards the dead redhead, "if not to murder Father Merry?"

"I do believe you're right, ma'am. They seek revenge for what he did to one of their own."

Folding her arms, the woman looked approvingly at her handiwork with the bandage. "And why are you seeking him?"

"I believe he might be able to help me. I'm seeking an old friend and partner who I believe passed this way."

"An old friend?"

"That's right. We have some… unfinished business."

"Business? I reckon I know your business. You're a bounty hunter, that's clear enough. This friend, he is a wanted man?"

"I can see there ain't much point me lying to you."

"No, that's for sure, mister. I've seen a lot since I arrived in this louse-ridden place and what I haven't seen, I can figure out for myself. Is he a bank robber?"

"No. A killer. The worst there is. It is my intention to bring him to justice, or kill him myself."

"For the money? Dear God, you're no better than him!"

Ritter blew out his lips. "Not just for the money, although I won't deny it will help my situation. No. It's more personal than that." He turned away and peered towards the distant hills, wondering again if a Henry rifle might be pointing directly at him. "He shot my brother stone dead, ma'am. I, too, am on the vengeance trail."

10

Some years before...

It was early 1871 and the cold wind cut to the bone when Chad Ritter paused on the porch of his sweetheart Diane's home and kissed her on the cheek.

She giggled. "Oh Chad, you are a darling, I have to say."

"You make me happy to be alive," he said, adjusting his hat for something to do, unable to meet her gaze, the heat rising along his jaw.

"Chad, being alive itself is a gift from God."

"I know it, but since I met you, my life has meaning. That is what I meant to say."

A shadow fell over them and Chad looked up to see Diane's father looming behind her, his great hands settling upon her shoulders. Impassive, he regarded Chad with eyes neither hard nor kind. And his voice, when he spoke, sounded sonorous. "Chad, you are welcome here anytime, so long as my daughter wishes it. You have courted her for three months now and I am gratified to hear your words."

"Thank you, sir, it's only my—"

"But your occupation concerns me, Chad. Sweeping out Frank Shepherd's boarding house is not a profession which inspires confidence in me for your future. If your intentions towards my daughter are honourable—"

"Daddy, *please*," interjected Diane, turning in her father's grip, "Chad is an honest and honourable man in every way."

"I am sure he is. But what security can he offer you?"

"We're not planning on marriage, Daddy." She turned a coy look towards Chad who stood awkwardly, shuffling his feet. As soon as Diane's father appeared, Chad had pulled off his hat and now held it tight to his chest, turning the brim through his hands as if it might give him some mode of protection. "At least, not yet, anyways."

"It's that 'not yet' which concerns me."

"Oh, Daddy..." She sighed deeply.

"What do you have to say for yourself, Chad?"

Clearing his throat, Chad took a deep breath, attempting to quell the nerves rattling around inside his sparse frame. "I do not intend to stay at the boarding house for much longer, Mr Hetherington, sir. I have already called upon Mrs Lomax—"

"The schoolmistress?"

"Yes, sir, the very same. She has agreed to give me some tuition in letters and numbers, sir. Her husband is the manager of the local bank, and he has assured me of a position as a clerk if my studies are successful."

"Well, I suppose that is something."

"You *see*, Daddy," cried Diane, beaming, "Chad is a responsible young man who has great potential."

The big man nodded, his mouth settling into a thin line. He pondered over Chad's words and, after a few moments, gave a grunt, a short nod and disappeared into the interior of the house.

"Oh my," gushed Diane, stepping forward to throw her arms around Chad. "Are you really going to Mrs Lomax for schooling?"

"I am," he said, holding her close. "It's what I want to do, Diane. For us. For our future. It's like I told you – I ain't ever felt this way before. My life feels complete."

"God bless you, Chad Ritter," and she turned her mouth to his and kissed him.

It was all he could do not to burst into great cries of joy as he skipped his way back to his tiny room at Frank Shepherd's boarding house.

Three days later, as Frank turned up the oil lamps dangling from the guest-house foyer's ceiling, Chad swept up the last remnants of the day's dust into the pan and tipped it into the galvanised bin which he took with him to every area he cleaned. He leaned on his broom and Frank stepped behind the reception desk to check the heavy, bound ledger sitting there. Settling a pair of pince-nez across the bridge of his nose, he opened the big book and ran a finger down the page before settling his stare upon his young employee.

"I have some out-of-towners calling this evening," he said. "Their range boss came to see me earlier to book the rooms. I wouldn't ordinarily board cowhands, being well experienced in their somewhat wild behaviour, but their boss paid top-dollar, so..." He drew in a deep breath. "Chad, I'm not expecting trouble, but it might be wise to remain in your room this evening, even if things do become rowdy. You understand me?"

"Well, yes I do, Mr Shepherd, but I have no intention of getting into any mischief with cowhands."

"No, I'm sure you haven't, but they can be unruly and impolite. I would not want an incident, that is all I'm saying."

"It was my intention to visit Miss Hetherington this evening. Her mother has invited me to dinner."

"Ah..." Frank chewed on his bottom lip, studying the names in the ledger with perhaps more concentration than was necessary. "Well, perhaps you could come in through the rear?"

Chad grunted, turned away and finished his last sweep before returning to the tiny room at the back where he kept all of his cleaning materials. He wondered why Shepherd should be so concerned about what might happen. Chad had never given him, nor anyone else for that matter, cause to suspect him of being a trouble-maker. It irked him that Shepherd's opinion might lean towards labelling him as such. Trying to put the conversation out of his mind, he busied himself with the last of his chores and then went to his room at the top of the house to prepare for his visit to Diane.

The wiry man dressed in a brown tweed suit slapped a bag of coins onto the table. "I have over one hundred dollars in gold, with another fifty or so in silver. I am here, gentlemen, to relieve you of yours." Roaring with laughter, he leaned back in his chair, thumbs stuck in his belt. With his jacket open, the Remington at his hip was clear to see.

"I beg to differ," said the large man opposite, spilling out the contents of his leather bag. "I have enough here to shame you into defeat, Hardin. Then, after we're done, I will bend over and you can kiss my sweet ass."

The four other men who were crammed around the table burst into guffaws at this, followed by much back-slapping and muttered comments, most of which the wiry man called Hardin ignored. "We shall see, Charley, we shall see."

Shepherd leaned over the reception desk and cleared his throat. "Boys, I have to remind you, this is not a saloon. Liquor is not readily on tap."

"Admonishment noted," said one of the others, the eldest of the group, who dipped down beneath the table and returned with a stone jar sporting four crudely drawn crosses upon its surface. "I have here some of the finest sour-mash this side of the Mississippi, aged in oak barrels and provided here for my good friends' partaking of."

More laughter. Hardin, grinning, looked towards Shepherd. "Would it be possible to provide us with glasses, sir? I do not much wish to swallow down the spittle of these good fellows, despite them being of noble character—"

"– yet questionable birth," put in Charley quickly and they all roared again.

Shepherd gave the group a hard look, knew there was not much he could do, sighed and pushed himself away from the desk. "I'll see what I can do."

He went into the back room just as Chad was coming down the steps. "Oh, sorry Mr Shepherd, but I'm just on my way to—"

"Don't hurry back, Chad," said Shepherd with a resigned air. "This evening is going to be long and will soon dissolve into chaos."

"They sound cheery enough."

"Oh, they are at the moment, but you mark my words, once some of them start losing their well-earned pieces of silver, they'll start a-cussin' and a-screamin'."

"They have already been paid?"

"They went to see a pony race just this side of Limestone County and some weedy-looking individual by the name of Hardin seems to have done himself well. Filled his boots, you might say."

"Limestone County? I heard things ain't so good over there, Mr Shepherd."

"There is marshal law there, yes, and it is not a place I would wish to take my grandmother to."

"Well, let's hope, Mr Shepherd, that they leave on the morrow, then we can get back to normal living."

Shepherd settled a studied gaze upon his young employee. "Chad, you are wise for your years. Let us get through this night without incident, then we can do exactly as you say."

Tipping his hat, Chad went out into the night, feeling he had gone some way towards altering Shepherd's opinion of him.

After their supper, which was punctuated with good conversation and high praise from Diane's mother, Chad took Diane out onto the porch, where they stood close, arms around one another, faces turned to the star-dappled sky. From somewhere in the distance, an owl made its presence felt and Diane sighed and pressed herself into his chest and murmured, "I wish every night could be as beautiful as this one."

"There's no reason why it can't be. When we have our own place, we can do just what we're doing now."

"You really think so?"

"Why not? We just need patience, that's all."

"Daddy said he spoke to Mr Lomax and discovered that what you said was true."

Stiffening slightly, Chad eased himself from her grip. "And why shouldn't it be?"

"Oh, don't start to fret none, Chad – Daddy just wants the best for me, is all. He is mightily impressed with your propriety, I can tell you that much."

Chad let out a long sigh. "I don't understand why people always think the worst of me. Old Shepherd, he more or less told me I was a hothead."

"He did not."

"He did too – telling me to stay out until his paying guests have all gone to bed. Do you know what they was doing when I came a-calling to you? Playing poker and drinking whiskey. And I'm the hothead!"

"Maybe he thought *they* was dangerous?"

"Nah, it's me he's worried about. Like your pa going to see Lomax – to check up on me!"

"Don't be put out by what he's done, Chad. He is pleased with you and the seriousness of your intentions."

"I know I ain't no well-schooled, clean-cut type, and that is why I is saying what I is saying. Your pa has never liked me. He has always—"

"No, that ain't so, Chad. He *does* like you. He just wants to be sure, is all."

"Sure of what? That I can provide for you? That I can keep you in the way you is accustomed?"

"Something like that. Don't be all put out by what he has said and done. He is pleased to find you a good and wholesome young man. He has given you his consent."

"He has?"

"Of course he has." She pulled him to her and this time there was no resistance on his part. "Now, let us just enjoy the moment. It is almost time for you to go."

He leaned forward and kissed her.

They walked down the long drive which led from Diane's impressive-looking house to the junction with the main road which led towards town. At the five-bar gate, he turned her into his arms and kissed her again. "I love you, Diane," he said softly, the words causing a lump to form in his throat. But he meant it. This night, dining with her parents, indulging in good conversation, in which he held his own and proved his intelligence and good breeding, had proven to him, if he needed any proving at all, that she was the girl for him.

"Hot diggerty, if she ain't a pretty one."

Chad froze solid and for a moment, he believed he had drifted into another world, a harder, much colder existence. He gazed into her large, oval eyes and knew it was true and he turned and saw them – three men, sporting chaps and six guns, and drunk.

"I do not believe I have seen anyone as pretty as she, don't you agree, boys?"

His two companions guffawed and mumbled their alcohol-laced agreement.

"What is your name, you little cutie, you?"

The house lay deep in shadow the tiny porch lamp barely able to pick out the figure of Diane's mother, but her shrill voice penetrated the night air. "Diane, you come back here now!"

Diane turned in his arms, whispering, "Who are they?"

Chad shrugged and turned to face them as they stood clearly out-lined by the moonlight. "What's it to you, boys?"

"What's it to us? Hell's bells, I think you do me an injustice, young fella."

The lead stranger took a step closer and Chad noted his twin guns, his surly swagger, the piece of straw hanging from his cruel, thin lips. A mass of brittle blond hair sprouted from beneath his hat and as he played with a strand above his right ear, his face split into a wide grin. "Are you doing me an injustice?"

"I'm merely asking what it is you want."

"Ah." The blond stuck his thumbs into his gun belt and rocked back-wards and forwards, arrogance oozing from every pore. "I was think-ing you was setting up to challenge me, boy."

"No, all I am asking, if you don't mind me repeating myself, is what is it you want?"

"With you? Nothing at all. But the pretty lady... now, she more than takes my fancy."

He made to take a step forward and immediately Chad positioned himself between Diane and the surly blond cowpoke.

"*Diane,*" shouted her mother again, her voice splintering, "*it's time for you to come in!*"

The cowhand leered, licking his lips. "Now boy, you is testing my patience."

But Chad stood his ground, even when the cowpoke's hand fell to the butt of one of his revolvers.

"I don't have a gun, mister," said Chad, flinching a little as Diane cowered behind him, tiny whimpers emitting from the back of her throat, "but I will fight you, make no mistake."

"Well now, what a hero you are."

"Chad, let's just go back inside," said Diane.

"Yes, Chad," said the cowpoke with a snigger, "why don't you go back inside. The lady and me have some business to attend to."

"Ah, hell, Guthrie," said one of the others from out of the darkness, "let's just leave these two love-birds alone. There's plenty more young things to be had in town."

"Yes, Guthrie," said another, "we don't need no trouble with the locals."

Chewing his bottom lip, Guthrie considered his companions' words, released a loud chuckle, then waggled his finger in front of Chad. "Boy, local or not, if I see you again, I'll give you a whuppin'."

"You can always try."

Grunting, Guthrie went to take another step, but a restraining hand clamped down onto his shoulder as one of his companions came up next to him. "Leave it, Guthrie. It's late. Let's get back and have a few drinks. We have an early start in the morning."

Grumbling under his breath, Guthrie reluctantly swaggered away, his eyes never leaving Chad's. One of the others doffed his hat towards Diane and soon they were swallowed up by the night, their loud cackling echoing through the darkness.

"Oh, my God," breathed Diane, sinking into Chad's chest, "what a horrible man."

"There's lots like him, darlin'. You get used to it."

"I don't think I would ever get used to someone like him."

"Well, you have no need to. He is gone now and, as one of them said, they are leaving tomorrow. So, no more need to worry."

"Would you have gotten into a fight with him, Chad?"

"To save your honour," he squeezed her tight, "I would fight the whole world."

Wandering along the main street of Archangel, Chad tried as best he could to keep thoughts of the vile Guthrie out of his mind, concentrating instead on the evening spent in the company of Diane and her parents. But, even with images of Diane's lovely, beaming face filling his mind, Guthrie always intervened – his snarling face, lips drawn back over chipped teeth, hand floating close to his gun. Perhaps if Chad himself sported a revolver, the consequences may have been considerably worse, for Chad felt sure the cowpoke was proficient with firearms, as well as his fists. A lifetime on the range would have taught him a whole encyclopaedia of tricks and moves and Chad, fitting his key into the rear entrance to the boarding house, felt that in the end, things had worked out for the best.

As he eased the door open, a burst of laughter greeted him from the dining room and he let loose a long sigh. This was what Shepherd had warned him about. Taking his time, he went to mount the wooden steps which led to his room at the top of the house.

The connecting door to the dining room opened wide and Shepherd came in, his mouth dropping open as he saw him. "Oh, Chad. Thank God!"

By opening the door and standing there, he was allowing those in the dining room a clear view into the little stock room.

And Chad, too, was able to look straight ahead and see the men gathered around a table, cards in hand, cigarettes smouldering, the whiskey jug doing its rounds.

But not just those who sat.

Those who were standing watching the game, too.

One of whom now fastened his hard stare on Chad.

"Ah, shit," breathed Chad.

Frowning, Shepherd looked from his young employee to the card-players in the room and back again. "What is it, Chad?"

Before Chad could give a reply, the wiry figure of Guthrie pushed past Shepherd, jaw jutting forward, thumbs in his gun belt, that swaggering arrogance all too obvious in the glare of the oil lamp dangling from the ceiling. "Well, well, if it ain't the lover-boy."

"What the hell is you doin', Guthrie?" came a voice from within.

"Finishing something, that's what."

Quickly, Shepherd threw up his hands. "Now listen, fella, I was given assurances there would be no trouble in my establishment."

"Oh, there won't be no trouble in here, mister," breathed Guthrie, his eyes narrowing as he stared into Chad's face. "Outside, boy. I'm about to teach you a lesson in manners."

"There ain't no need for that, mister," said Chad, unable to keep the fear from his voice.

"You was full of gusto in front of your little girl, but you ain't so big and brave now, are you, boy?"

Guthrie took a step closer, but Shepherd put out his hand to stop him. Snarling, Guthrie dashed the hand away. Shepherd was a big man, but his fighting days were long behind him and Guthrie was well-schooled. His right fist swung short and sharp into the hotel owner's ribs. Shepherd's breath erupted in a blast and he buckled and fell to his knees, retching loudly.

Chad came off the steps at a rush, anger overcoming his fear as well as his good sense. His fists came up and he threw a wild left, which Guthrie easily dipped under. The cowpoke swung a vicious uppercut which connected under Chad's chin, lifted him off his feet and sent him smashing against the backroom door. The old, warped timbers gave way and Chad fell into the night and lay sprawled on the ground, senses stunned by the blow.

From somewhere on the limits of his consciousness, he heard voices, some of them gloating, others shouting, pleading. Maybe one was Shepherd's.

"My God, that's enough! He's only a boy."

Another, sneering, almost certainly Guthrie's. "He's gonna pay for dishonouring me."

And another, casual, soft, but all the more terrifying for it. "Leave it now, Guthrie – your pride is gonna get you killed one of these days."

But then they all merged into one formless clump of entangled noise as Chad's head swam and he felt hot, sticky goo trickling from the back of his skull.

Shepherd, still reeling, managed to stagger over to Chad and lift him up in his arms. "Ah, God damn, he cracked his head on a stone here." He swung his face towards the men gathered in the dimly lit doorway. "God damn you, you bastard."

Face contorted into a demonic scowl of rage, Guthrie leaped on the hotel owner, picked him up by the throat and butted him full in the nose.

Falling back, Shepherd collapsed in the dirt, dazed, the blood dripping from his broken nose. For a moment, not much made sense as images danced around in front of him and he thought he saw Chad getting unsteadily to his feet.

"Chad," managed Shepherd, "Chad, you just sit right down and let all this pass."

"I can't do that, Mr Shepherd."

He saw Chad grip Guthrie by the shoulder and turn him. A solid left connected with the man's jaw and he staggered backwards, amazed at the young man's audacity.

"Chad," said Shepherd, struggling to his feet, "that's enough now."

"The hell it is."

But then Guthrie had his gun in his hand and he was grinning. "You sonofabitch. No one lands a sucker punch on me, you little bastard."

"Guthrie," said the wiry man, whom Shepherd remembered had won handsomely at the pony races, "put the gun away before you do something stupid."

"Fuck you, Hardin, you streak of piss. You'll not tell me what to do."

Guthrie turned, the gun still there, but now pointing towards the man he'd called Hardin. Hardin merely sighed and pulled back his coat. The others, who by now had spilled out into the street, all stepped away, some muttering words of caution to both men, but mainly to Guthrie.

"Give it up, Guthrie, or, so help me, I'll put you in the ground."

"Like hell! You ain't even got your gun drawn," Guthrie cackled. "I'll kill you first, then these two bastards."

"No, you won't. We is leaving this alone, and we is leaving it alone now."

Guthrie's gun hand came up, squeezing off several shots, none of which struck home. Hardin returned the favour, his Colt barking loud in the night air.

Shepherd later recounted to the local newspaper how both men could not have been more than fifteen paces apart, yet the shots mainly went wide. Guthrie received a round in the gut and fell. Chad, who was now exposed to fire as Guthrie crumpled, took the next two shots full in the chest.

With both men down, an awful silence fell, broken only by Hardin spilling out spent cartridges onto the ground. Once reloaded, he stepped up to Guthrie. The blond cowpoke glanced upwards, pleading, "Please, John, don't shoot me no more."

But Hardin did. A single bullet between the eyes.

And then it was over.

11

1873, two years after Chad's death.

"My good Lord in Heaven, that is an awful story."

"Yes, it is. Hardin murdered my brother in cold blood, and he shall pay with his life for what he done."

They rode side by side, she on the redhead's horse and Ritter on his. As he rode, he took in the surrounding countryside, feeling torn between explaining more to this woman who had almost killed him, and letting his explanation stew. In the end, he blew out a blast of breath and reined in his horse. She stopped, fixing him with a quizzical stare whilst he rifled in his saddlebags. Pulling out an oily wrapper, he opened it with something like reverence and thrust a neatly folded piece of newsprint towards her.

"I can't read all the words, but here is the whole thing, written down for the newspapers. Shepherd, the boarding house owner, told it all as he saw it." He waggled it in front of her. "Read it if you don't believe me."

"I never said I *didn't* believe you."

"Even so."

After a moment's hesitation, she reached out and unfolded the paper and read through it. Ritter waited patiently.

He watched her. Her bottom lip screwed up and she muttered to herself in low tones as she read. Tilting her head, she said aloud, "It says here, '*And I knew it was the gunfighter Hardin, for all his associates called him so. One told him he should run, as a posse would be sure to string him up. So he took flight on his horse and the others ran. As far as I know, I am the only one who has stepped forward to put down what happened that fateful night. It also fell to me to tell Chad's betrothed and that is something I do not wish to endure ever again, for she was heartbroken by the news and, even now, spends most of her days weeping for her lost love.'* "

She sat astride her horse in silence for a long time before carefully refolding the paper and slipping it inside the wrapper once more. "That is quite awful." She thrust out her hand and Ritter took the paper and returned it to his saddlebag. "I'm not all that sure what killing this Hardin will do, however. No good will come of it."

"It will make me rest a darn sight easier, ma'am."

"Are you sure of that?"

"As sure as I can be of anything in this uncertain world of ours."

"Well, I must confess I would be a might more comfortable with the idea of you turning him in to face justice, rather than meting it out yourself."

"That's the way I do things."

"That may well be so, but it doesn't mean it's right."

"An eye for an eye and all that – you know the Bible and that's what it says."

"Does it? And when was the last time you read it?"

Grimacing, Ritter turned away and studied the trail ahead. At one hundred paces or so, it veered away to the right, and a left fork meandered on towards the town. "Which way do we go to get to the Parker place?"

"The right. It cuts around town and crosses to several outlying farms and homesteads. There's no guarantee the Father is still there."

"I reckon he'll choose to stand there and wait for that redhead's *compadres* to arrive." He gave her a lingering look. "Aren't you anxious to make sure he's still alive?"

A slight reddening developed around her jawline and for the first time he noted her usual assuredness giving way to uncertainty, even fear. He realised in that moment that this curious woman, so willing to nearly put him in the grave, had an emotional connection with the good Father.

"What are you smirking at?"

Ritter gave a start, her harsh, accusing tone bringing him up sharp. "I'm not," he said quickly.

Unconvinced, she flicked her reins and the dead redhead's horse obediently moved forward. Watching her back for some moments, and liking what he saw, Ritter pushed up alongside her and together, they ambled down the trail to the right, without another word passing between them until they reached their destination – the Parker ranch.

12

Rolling his shoulders under the coarse material of his habit, Father Merry went to the tiny stove crammed into the far corner of the room and busied himself with swilling out coffee grounds before setting a fresh pot on the flame. He caught a sharp intake of breath from Nati behind him and he turned. She stood looking through the single hatch beside the main door. He went to her and settled his hand on her slim shoulder. "What is it?"

"Riders," she said, the single word sending a chill through the priest. He bent forward and followed the direction of her gaze.

Without a word, Nati swept up the Spencer carbine and checked it for the umpteenth time.

"Two," said Merry, calculating the odds. "Not what I was expecting."

"Perhaps more have skirted round back. I may not have heard them."

"You've been looking for their approach keenly enough. I think this is all there is."

Grunting dismissively, Nati went to the door to pull up the bar.

"What are you doing?"

"I'm going to go out and see what they want."

"What if it's a trap?"

"I'll plug 'em first, don't you worry, Father."

Shaking his head, Merry stepped up beside her, his revolver materialising in his hand. "Best let me." He smiled. "You cover me from the window. You have better range than me, and your aim will be far more certain if you use the ledge."

"And if I suspect anything?"

"I'll shout, and then you plug 'em."

Despite the tense atmosphere, she smiled. "God go with you, Father."

He kissed his first two fingers and pressed them against her forehead before raising the bar and stepping outside.

Blinking in the harsh, afternoon sunlight, he took a few paces to his right, which would allow Nati a clear shot from the hatch if the need arose. As he watched the riders' approach, however, he wasn't all that sure if such an event would be necessary. Frowning, he studied the approaching couple and felt his throat go dry.

"Oh, sweet Jesus," he said, "it's Grace!"

Before Nati could give a meaningful interjection, Merry broke into a run, all thoughts of personal safety gone in an instant.

Mouth splitting into a wide, gaping grin, he saw her jump down from the saddle, her face alight with joy. Already, his arms were spreading to welcome her but, as they ran towards one another, he glanced at the other rider, noted the half-mocking smile he wore and something flickered across his memory. He recognised the tall, rangy stranger, but from where, he could not determine.

And then she was in his arms, laughing uproariously. He swung her around and around, his mouth fastening on hers and suddenly nothing else in the world mattered.

"Oh, dear God, I thought I'd never see you again," she gasped, pressing her face into his barrel chest.

He held her close, his cheek resting on the top of her head. He dwarfed her and the feel of her in his embrace sent a pulse of desire through his entire being.

"Not wishing to impose on you two love-birds," said the stranger with a chuckle, "but I think we need to prepare ourselves for what is coming, padre."

Still holding her, Merry turned his gaze to the stranger, who had now crossed one leg over the other as he sat astride his horse and was nonchalantly rolling himself a cigarette with tobacco taken from a small pouch hanging from his saddle. Narrowing his eyes, Merry took in the tied-down gun and the sand-coloured cord coat which, like the rest of his apparel, appeared encrusted with a thick layer of dust. Most of Merry's attention, however, centred on a livid red scar which poked out from beneath the man's sweat-stained neckerchief. "Do I know you?"

"We ain't been formally introduced," said the stranger, sticking the cigarette into his mouth, "but we sort of stumbled into one another when you beat the living shit out of some fat bastard back in town." He grinned, struck a match across his thigh and lit his smoke.

"That still doesn't tell me who you are." Without ever taking his eye from the stranger, Merry gently moved Grace to one side, revealing the revolver in his hand.

Blowing out a stream of smoke, the stranger nodded towards Merry's gun. "Don't be getting it into your head you can use that thing on me, padre," he said, tossing away the spent match. "It would be a great pity to have to kill you, especially as I believe you have some news to give me."

"Patrick," said Grace in a low voice, her slight hands closing around Merry's, "this man saved me from being molested by the most horrible man I've ever met."

Merry pursed his lips, taking in the way the stranger's hand appeared so relaxed, and so far from his gun. Surely it would not take much to put a bullet into him. "He's a gunfighter."

"No," said the man on the horse, "I'm what is affectionately termed a 'bounty hunter'. My name is Gus Ritter, and I'm searching for the bastard who killed my brother." He leaned forward, his gaze piercing. "You can tell me where he is, so Wilbur told me back in the saloon. But, if I figure rightly, that fat slob's friends will be coming here to take their vengeance out on you, and I'm here to prevent that. In the meantime, you need to tell me where John Wesley Hardin went."

Frowning, Merry very slowly returned his revolver to its hiding place underneath his habit, snaked his arm around Grace's shoulders and pulled her close. "You help me, I'll help you."

"Now, that is a fair deal, padre." Ritter sat up straight and quietly smoked his cigarette.

"How long do you think we have?"

"Difficult to say. But long enough to get ready. They'll be sending a small army here, padre. But I reckon once we take off the head, the rest of the beast will high-tail it back to wherever it is that it came from."

"That'll be the Scrimshaw ranch."

"You let me know who he is, and I'll kill him."

"You're more than a bounty hunter, mister. You're a stone-cold killer."

"I'm a lot of things, padre, most of which you don't want to know. But I will do whatever is necessary to put Hardin in the ground." He took a last pull on his cigarette and threw it away. "So, let's get our welcoming committee ready."

13

Accompanied by five well-armed and angry looking cowhands, Mario rode from his father's ranch across the open range towards Reece, who waited, chewing his lip anxiously. Without any hint of a greeting, Mario reined in his horse and sat there, breathing hard. He spent a long time studying his brother, his stare unblinking and cold, before turning his head to look at Tobias who sat slumped against a cluster of rocks, eyes closed, face swollen, groaning. "He looks bad."

"He *is* bad."

"Then why in the hell haven't you taken him to Doc Wilson's?"

"That was my intention."

"So what happened?"

"Jessup. He took it upon himself to take matters into his own hands, so to speak."

"What in the hell does that mean?"

To even the most casual of glances, it would be apparent this speaker was not like the others. Not only in his attire, which comprised almost entirely of black garments, nor the twin revolvers holstered at his hip, butts turned inwards, but in his ice-cold stare which seemed to freeze the very soul of any who gazed upon him. Reece felt it now and, despite his best efforts, experienced an unsettling churning within his stomach. He tried to hold the speaker's gaze, but failed and looked away, deflated. "He rode off."

"Rode off? You mean you angered him?"

Reece snapped his head up, defiant, features distorted with a furious scowl. "No! I told him not to go off and confront the priest, but he did so, nevertheless."

"And why didn't you go with him?"

"I was asleep."

"*Asleep?*" The man inched his horse forward, his face hard, eyes bright, burning with a furious rage.

"Hold on there, Martindale," said Mario quickly.

Without checking his advance, Martindale ignored Mario's command and sidled up alongside Reece, who wilted under his stare. "You fell asleep and he slipped away?"

"That's about it."

"So, not only do you not take poor old Toby here to the Doc's, but you haven't got the sand to go and confront this shit-holed priest for yourself."

"It's not that," said Reece, sounding as desperate as he felt, "I told you. Jessup snuck off and I was tired of waiting." He looked over to his brother. "Tired of waiting on *you*."

"Oh, so all of this is my fault?" Mario leaned back in his saddle and shook his head. "It might be of interest to you, Reece, but I have spent almost all of my time trying to calm Pa down after what you said to him."

"*What I said to him?* You've got that all the wrong way round, Mario."

"Mmmm... well, once we've sorted out this little scuffle with the priest, you can tell me what has got Pa so fired up he won't even have you in the house no more."

"He's opposed to going up against the priest," said Reece quickly. "And that fits in with what the barkeep in the saloon said when Jessup and me went to fetch Toby from town."

"*What* did the barkeep say?" said Martindale scathingly, mouth turned up at the corner in a sneer.

"That I should be careful."

"Careful? Of a priest?" Martindale swivelled in his saddle towards the others. "Afraid of a man of God are we, Reece? A man who spends all his days swaggering around in a dress, telling us all how to live our lives? He ain't nothing but a bag of wind, Reece." He turned again towards the Scrimshaw boy. "You is scared of him?"

"There's something about him, Martindale... something which doesn't fit with who he is supposed to be. I been thinking – how can a simple priest do what he did to Toby, eh? A man of God, like you say, ain't equipped to dish out such a beating."

"It's true he's a big man," put in Mario, turning to gaze across the range. "Maybe Jessup has saved us all a lot of trouble by ending all of this here and now. When did he leave?"

"I'm not rightly sure, me falling asleep and all."

Martindale blew out a sharp breath and Mario gestured to one of the others. "Francie, I want you to take Toby into town and get him patched up over at Doc Wilson's. The rest of us will head out to the church, which is where I'm guessing the priest is right now."

"Unless he has high-tailed out," said Martindale.

"He knew what the consequences would be," said Reece. "I'm not thinking he is a coward."

"Then he'll die," said Martindale.

"Yes, he will," said Reece and, with an emphatic flick of his reins, he pulled his horse around and spurred it in the direction of the church.

14

An eerie silence lay over the church and its surroundings. Except for the birds, of course. A squabbling bunch, flapping and pecking at one another, trying to get the choicest morsels from the prostrate and bloody corpse lying there. The riders stopped and watched in stupefied horror.

"What in the hell has gone on here?" said someone.

All of a sudden, Martindale shot one of the feasting buzzards and the rest erupted skywards in a mass of terrified squawking. "I hate them damn things," he muttered, holstering his revolver.

"Move around both sides," said Mario to the others. "Reece, you go through the front."

"I'll do that," said Martindale, easing himself down from the saddle. "The rest of you move real easy."

As the black-clothed gunfighter sauntered across to the half-eaten corpse, Mario shot Reece a look. "You think that could be Merry?"

"If it is, then where the hell is Jessup?"

"I don't like this," said Mario, lifting himself up from the saddle to stretch his legs. "I'm thinking your suspicions about the padre are correct, Reece."

Gnawing his lip, Reece nodded as he watched Martindale step up to the prone body and toe it with his boot. He saw the gunman's head fall and said, "That dead-un ain't the padre."

Whirling around, Martindale screwed up his face and yelled, "That bastard has done for Jessup!"

"Then we find him," returned Mario and looked again at his brother. "Where do you think he has gone? I reckon north – as far away from here as he can get."

"Nah, I don't buy it. He's not the kind to run. He beat Toby because of the girl. Flo Parker. If he's anywhere, he'll be there, at the young girl's place."

"You know where it is?"

"Nope. But we can always—"

"I know where it is," said Martindale, coming up fast. He swung himself into his saddle. "That girl's sister, Nati, she is a looker. Me, Jessup and Toby, we been callin' on them two gals for some time now. If it wasn't for—"

"Just a goddamned moment there," snapped Mario, the blood draining from his face. "You mean to say you and Toby have visited the Parker place before?"

"That's what I just said, didn't I?"

"And did you know about Toby taking advantage of the younger one?"

"Taking advantage? Shit, Mario, she was cock-teasing us all from the start."

"She's thirteen," said Reece, in a low voice laced with disbelief.

"I've been with whores younger than her," said Martindale, with a cackle. "Damn, if you went down to El Paso, you'd find yourself up to your—"

"Martindale," interjected Mario, "you could have saved us all a lot of aggravation if you'd have kept that fucking idiot Toby in check. I can't believe you knew about all of this."

"I didn't know the goddamned preacher would kick Toby almost to death, did I, you ass!" With his face turning crimson, the gunman turned and spat. "Fuck you, Mario, trying to be all self-righteous when you ain't nothing but a scoundrel yourself. And *you*," he jabbed his finger at Reece, "you ain't ever gonna be the man your pappy is. He has more sand in his fucking piss than you have in your whole goddamned scrawny hide."

"You watch your mouth," said Reece, body rigid with rage. "Just remember who pays your wages."

"I remember – and it ain't you."

"Just calm down," said Mario, leaning across to give his horse's neck a gentle pat. Just like the others, the animal was unnerved by the sharp exchanges between the men. "What's done is done, I guess. But I ain't happy, Martindale. None of this had to come this far, and now Jessup's dead and we have to go fetch that preacher and string him up."

"I'm gonna kill him," said Martindale.

"No," Mario said quickly, "no, we make him *pay* for what he's done. We hang him from a tree and watch the miserable bastard choke to death."

Grunting, Martindale nodded, convinced by Mario's words. "All right, but first I want to slice off his balls with my knife. I want him to go through an eternity of pain before he dies, you get me?"

"I get you."

"Then let's get to it."

As he went to turn his horse, Reece put in, "What about Jessup – shouldn't we bury him? Say a few words?"

Chuckling, Martindale shook his head. "He won't be hearing any words, and where he's gone I doubt if he'll have the time to listen. He's already in hell, Reecey boy, roasting in the pit, and those vultures may as well pick him clean for all I care."

"I thought he was your friend."

"He was, but now he's dead – and there it is."

15

Doc Wilson ordered his boy, Norbert, to carry Toby Scrimshaw into his surgery. Norbert was a huge man who picked up his charge as if he were a mere child. Watching him, Francie shook his head, disgust written across his face. "Why do you have a goddamned nigger working for you, Doc?"

About to turn and go into his surgery, Wilson stopped in his tracks and swung round. "What did you say?"

"A goddamned negro slave? Why can't you employ a good, honest white man?"

"Like you, you mean?"

"Like me? Hell, I already got a job, and I don't need no—"

"For your information, you ignorant, cloth-eared bastard, Norbert is ten times more honest and hard-working than most of the unworthy trash living round these parts."

Francie's mouth fell open. "What did you call me?"

"I'm calling you ignorant, because that is what you are. Norbert does his duties better than most, and in return he gets board and lodging. I need a good, strong man to do my portering, as so many are dying round these parts what with scarlet fever and diphtheria. He has the strength of a bear, and I need him."

"I ain't ignorant and you have no right to call me that."

"You *is* ignorant, and prejudiced to boot."

"If I had not been instructed to seek out your services, I would shoot you dead here and now for how you have spoken to me."

Wilson tilted his head. "I knew your parents, Francis Bell, and they would be turning in their graves if they could hear you right now. Go about your business before I lose my temper."

"You ain't nothing but a petered-out old man, but you have wronged me and I will seek satisfaction from you when you have patched up poor old Toby." He stuck his thumbs in his belt and jutted his chin forward. "And that's a promise."

With a jaunty flick of his head, Francie spun around and strutted off without a backward glance.

Crossing the main street, Francie made a bee-line for the only open saloon and marched inside.

The room, well-lit by two pairs of windows on either side of the batwing doors, was large and sparsely furnished, just a few tables pushed into the far corner. Around one of these, a group of bedraggled-looking men were playing at cards. Several others leaned against the bar counter, contemplating their drinks. The barkeep, a big-boned, florid-looking man, shirt sleeves rolled up way past his thick biceps, had his back to the room counting bottles. Francie rapped on the counter with a dollar piece and the barkeep turned, arching a single eyebrow. "Whisky."

With a grunt, the barkeep selected a thick-bottomed glass and tipped in a measure from the bottle he fetched from the shelf. He slid the whisky over. "That dollar will get you another three of those."

Nodding, Francie drained the glass in one and proffered it for a fill-up. "Is this where my partner was beat up by the priest?"

The barkeep stopped in the process of filling the glass and gave Francie a questioning look. "Are you one of the Scrimshaw boys? They came here and took their friend out."

"I know. I've come back with him to see the doc."

"He's still in a bad way?"

"You could say that." Francie watched as the whisky sloshed up to the rim of the glass, then swept it up and downed a mouthful. He spluttered then coughed, pressing the back of his hand against his mouth. "That tastes like horse-piss."

"It's the best there is. My supplier ships it in from New York."

"Well, there you have it – that's Yankee horse-piss."

"We don't talk of such things here, mister. For us, the War is over."

"My pa and his two brothers were with Picket and none of 'em came back. That gives me reason to hate every last one of those Yankees."

"I feel for that, mister. I lost my own brother in the War, at Fredericksburg. But we can't keep hating."

"Oh? Why not?"

Blowing out his cheeks, the barkeep shrugged and turned away, leaving the bottle beside Francie's glass. Francie spent a long time staring at the whisky, before pouring a refill and swinging across the room to where the men were playing their game.

"What's this?"

Nobody looked up, all of them studying their cards with great intensity. One of them shuffled in his chair, cleared his throat and said, "Seven-up."

Nodding, Francie pulled out a chair. "Mind if I join you?"

Sitting across the table, a wiry-looking man with a handle-bar moustache ran his tongue across his top lip. "As long as you have money."

"I have."

"Then feel free – after this hand is done."

Francie watched the game play out in silence, noting how the man with the moustache confidently flipped and chose his cards with an almost dismissive air, as if he were well schooled in the game and knew all of its many vagaries. At no point did he look up. His eyes remained fixed on what he was doing and when he spread out his card hand with a theatrical flourish, the others gasped and groaned, throwing themselves back in their chairs, exasperated.

"Goddamn, how do you win all of the time?" said one, counting out the last few coins he had left in his hand. "Shit, you have cleaned me out."

Raking in the stash of coins and torn bills in the centre of the table, the moustachioed man merely grinned and nodded. "It's called skill. It ain't for nothing they named me the Seven-Up Kid some years back."

Pulling up his chair, Francie leaned forward as the moustachioed man shuffled the cards. They were old and well creased, the corners torn and curled up.

"They your cards, mister?"

Not pausing in his sorting of the cards, the moustachioed man grunted his affirmation.

The barkeep appeared, offering the men refills of whisky. "When will your friend be fixed up?"

Frowning at the barkeep, Francie looked up and said, "As soon as he is ready."

"Doc gave no indication? He was beat up real bad."

"I knows it. I took him there myself. But I'll be going back." He snapped his head around as cards were flicked in his direction. He studied the way the moustachioed man dealt them. "That doc of yours has a scathing mouth on him and that's for sure."

"What does that mean?"

"That he insulted me." He waited whilst the man to the left of the dealer chose a card from the stash. With a disgusted huff, he threw it onto the discard pile.

"Insulted you? Doc Wilson? That don't seem hardly possible – the man is a gentleman. I've known him for years and never heard anyone say a bad thing about him."

"Well, you have now," said Francie, as the second man also threw away a card. "I aim to visit him later on and teach him some manners."

The barkeep gave a sharp laugh. "Well, I'd be a mite careful there, son. Doc Wilson served in the Mexican *and* the Civil Wars. He boxed for his regiment. Never known him to fall."

Francie pursed his lips and watched the third player slip his chosen card into his hand and place another on the pile. "I ain't planning on fisticuffs."

"Then what *is* you planning?"

Francie drew a card and studied it. His eyes roamed to the man opposite. "Something more permanent."

"Then you is a fool, mister."

Studying his hand, Francie picked out a queen and snapped it on top of the discard pile. "He said something similar and I aim to kill him for it. If I were you," he leaned back and studied the barkeep from toe to head, "I'd keep a civil tongue in my head, 'cepting you is maybe also looking for trouble."

"Mister, you is not the sort of guest I want here in my establishment, so if you'd—"

"Oh, hush now, Wilbur," said the moustachioed dealer, smiling thinly at the barkeep, "can't you see we are trying to play our game?"

"I do see that, but I would gracefully request that this here—"

"This here *gentleman* is trying to concentrate."

Francie's frown grew deeper as he stared hard at the moustachioed man. "What is you inferring?"

"I ain't inferring nothing, boy. But you seem a touch tense and have something of a grudge against the whole goddamned world. My advice... play the damned game."

Something changed in the air at that moment. Slowly, one by one, the other players dropped their cards and eased back their chairs. Francie studied them, noting how their faces had gone the colour of chalk. No one spoke. "I will play it," said Francie quietly, looking down at his hand, "but first of all, you tell me why these here cards are marked the way they are."

Someone drew in their breath sharply. Another half-rose and the third leaned forward, his hand about to touch Francie's forearm before a sharp glance from the cowhand caused him to pause. "Mister, you have no cause to say that. We've been playing with John here for a few weeks now and we is all satisfied as to his honesty and good sportsmanship."

"Is that a fact?"

"Yes, it is."

"Then tell me, how many times have you won against him," Francie threw down his cards, "with him using that there deck?"

"Mister, I don't think you should be—"

"Shut up, Clancy," said the moustachioed man, whose own hand of cards was splayed out in front of him in both hands.

"John, I was only trying to—"

"I *said...* shut up." Grinning, the man called John carefully placed the cards face-up on the table. Everyone looked, including Francie. He counted the cards and there they were, from Ace to Seven, set out in a neat line. "Like I said, I am known as the Seven-Up Kid. Perhaps you have heard of me?"

Wilbur coughed. "I think we should all take a break."

But nobody moved. Nobody hardly dared breathe. Over at the counter, the men who had been drinking there quietly slipped out of the bar, the hinges on the batwing door creaking painfully in their wake.

Wilbur tried another cough. "I have had enough trouble here, gentlemen, I don't want no more."

"I think your hope for a period of peaceful contemplation and congeniality is somewhat premature," said John evenly, eyes fixed on the cowhand seated opposite him.

"I know what I saw," said Francie, through clenched teeth. "My only relief is that I did not lose any money to you, unlike these poor saps here."

"Spit it out, boy."

"I ain't your boy."

"Spit it out."

Taking a breath, Francie shoved back his chair and stood up. "You're a goddamned card-sharp. I recognised you for what you were the moment I sat down, with those filthy cards and their tears and turned-down corners. I've met your kind on every trail I've ever been on and I ain't got no stomach for you, or anyone like you. Now stand up, you slit-eyed bastard and give back the money you swindled from these here gentlemen, or I'll plug you where you sit."

"I is tooled, boy."

"Don't call me *boy*," snarled Francie and went to pull his gun.

Everything happened quickly from that point. Before Francie's gun had cleared its holster, the man called John shot him through the throat, sending him spinning and floundering like a man lost in fog. Gun falling, hands clasping at the wound, his life-blood pumping from between his fingers, Francie gurgled and spluttered, fell to his knees and tried to squeal.

"Oh, good God Almighty," cried Wilbur, backing off towards the counter as the other men scrambled for the exit, mindless of the squirming, dying cowhand spewing blood on the saloon floor.

"This was not my intention," said John in a tired voice, stepping around the table to stand over the stricken cowhand, "but I will not be wronged or aggrieved by false witness." He brought up his pistol and put a bullet into Francie's head and the horrible gargling noise from his mouth stopped at last.

"Sweet Jesus."

John dropped the spent cartridges onto the floor and replaced them with fresh ones from his belt. "Who the hell was he, anyway?"

Wilbur's only response was a feeble shake of the head.

"Well, that's about all he's worth." He tossed a silver dollar towards the trembling barkeep. "That'll cover his burial. Nothing too elaborate, mind, as he wasn't worth more than a handful of shit."

Clearing his throat, Wilbur grasped one of the abandoned whisky bottles on the bar, pressed it against his mouth and drank deeply. Then, gasping harshly, he stood and stared, still shaking. "My God. I ain't ever seen anything like that in my whole life."

Shrugging, John drew his tailcoat around him and pointed at the corpse. "Nor, do I suggest, has he." He grinned. "Or should that be, *had* he?" He chuckled.

"What about his friend over at Doc Wilson's? Once he gets wind of what's happened, he'll—"

"Ah yes, the one beaten up by Father Merry."

"Hell, you *know* the priest?"

"For quite some time, yes." Another grin, much wider this time. "He hasn't always been a priest."

"Then you should know that this here cowpoke and others like him want Merry dead for what he done to the other one over at the Doc's."

"I see. Well…" he put both hands into the small of his back and leaned back, stretching out his muscles, "it is not my desire to be hunted by another posse of outraged friends and relatives, so I shall pay the other a visit over at the surgery, then find a way of ending all of this before it even starts."

He touched the brim of his hat with a forefinger and went out into the scalding hot day.

16

Drying his hands on an old, threadbare towel, Doc Wilson came out of his surgery and stopped when he saw the slightly built man in the dark-coloured tailcoat, pin-striped trousers and frilled shirt standing at the end of the hallway.

The stranger was grinning. "Howdy," he greeted him.

"Can I help you with anything, mister?" asked Wilson, drying his hands with deliberate slowness now, his eyes locked on those of the stranger.

"Could be. You have a patient, under your care – big man, badly beaten."

"Yes, I do. Is he … a friend of yours?"

"No, not exactly. I believe he had a companion, however. A companion who brought him here?"

"Yes." Wilson took the towel and folded it neatly. "A most objectionable gentleman who took umbrage at something I said."

"An insult?"

"He took it as such, although it was not meant. I believe he has a mind to return and shoot me dead."

The stranger's smile widened. "Well, I'm here to tell you he won't be bothering you, or anyone else for that matter, ever again."

Wilson frowned, letting the words percolate through his mind. "I see."

"I'm not quite sure you do, but nevertheless, I have a favour to ask. May I visit your patient? I need to ask him a question."

"He's not up to talking. I suspect his jaw is broke."

"Ah." The stranger shrugged. "Then perhaps you might help. I'm looking for the whereabouts of the man who beat up your patient. The priest, so I'm led to believe – Father Merry."

"I'm not quite sure I should—"

"Oh, you can. Trust me." The man smiled. "I'm a friend."

"A friend of Father Merry? He is a singularly private man, although well liked. Could I ask you your name, sir?"

"You may."

Wilson waited, but as it became obvious the stranger was not about to reveal his identity, he asked again.

The stranger smiled. "Hardin. John Hardin."

"I'm pleased to know you, Mr Hardin." After brief consideration, Wilson gently folded up the towel and placed it on a small table set against the hallway wall. "Perhaps one question will be all right, I suppose. But if he becomes restless or distressed, I'll have to ask you to—"

"He'll be fine."

Following the doctor's lead, the stranger went into the small, airy surgery where a large, bloated man lay stretched out on a narrow bed, the lower part of his head swathed in bandages. As Hardin drew closer, the man's eyes flickered open. Despite them being swollen and badly bruised, they flared as he recognised his visitor. He grunted, instinctively pushing himself away, which caused him to wince.

"He knows you?"

Hardin shrugged. "Our paths have crossed, yes. He is the son of a local cattle rancher called Scrimshaw. I used to work for him some time ago."

"I thought I recognised you..."

A thin smile spread across Hardin's face. "I left under something of a gathering storm cloud, Doctor. Young Tobias here and I crossed swords." He leaned towards the stricken patient. "Just nod, Toby. Merry did this to you?"

At first, Toby did not react, except for those eyes, wide and wild.

Hardin sighed and his face grew hard. "Toby, I'm not here to seek my vengeance for what you did to me. That can wait. Right now, I want to go and help the good Father. He helped me. It's my turn to help him."

The doctor cleared his throat. "I can tell you the direction to his church."

Turning, Hardin nodded his thanks to Wilson's offer. He looked again at Toby. "Was it Merry, Toby?" At last, a brief nod. "And your boys are out to pay him a visit?" Another nod. Hardin straightened. "This sonofabitch accused me of stealing wages from the rest of the boys whilst they slept in the bunkhouse. They rounded on me and beat me – but they did not find the money, because this bastard was the one who took it."

Toby stiffened, trying to raise himself from the bed, strangulated croaks squeezing out from his clenched teeth. Placing the flat of his hand on the cowboy's chest, Hardin pressed him back down. "They almost beat me to death before the priest interceded and saved me. I don't forget kindness, nor do I forget being wronged." At this juncture, he pressed his hand down more harshly and Toby squealed.

"That's enough," snapped Wilson, rushing forward and knocking Hardin's hand away. Toby fell back, eyes closed, head rolling, in obvious discomfort. "I'd like you to leave now, Mr Hardin."

"How long is he going to wallow here, Doc?"

"As long as it takes."

"That's no answer."

"It's the only one you're going to get. Now, get out of my surgery, Mr Hardin. And don't come back."

Tilting his head, Hardin gave another one of those slick smiles. "Oh, I'll be back, Doctor Wilson. And when I do, you'd better not stand in my way. You get Toby fit enough to stand and pull a gun, because destiny is bringing all of this to closure, and I wouldn't want you to be a victim of the fallout."

"Like I say, Mr Hardin – leave."

"Which direction is the church?"

"I have a mind not to tell you. Nothing good is going to come of any of this."

"Of that you can be certain. Fortunately, I think I can remember the way. But thank you, anyway."

And with that, Hardin spun on his heels and went outside, mounted his horse and cantered out of town, ignoring the many fearful looks from the passers-by.

17

Pulling up their horses, the group of riders peered across the open scrub towards the tiny farmhouse. It appeared deserted and the silence was total. Rubbing his jaw, Mario took a moment to look around before grunting, "They've gone."

"You don't know that for sure," hissed Martindale. "They could be cowering inside, like the mangy curs they are."

"There's a young girl in there," said Reece, "in case you have forgotten – the one Toby raped."

"I ain't forgotten nothing," said Martindale. "All I care about is that priest. I want him strung up by his balls before this afternoon is out."

"What if he has high-tailed it?"

"Then I'll track him down. He can't have got far. But first, we check the house." He gestured to two of the cowpokes, "Skirt round to the left, nice and slow. When you reach that scattering of rocks and boulders yonder, set yourselves down and cover the front and back. If anyone breaks cover, you shoot 'em dead."

"Even if they is women?"

Martindale turned to face the scrawny cowpoke who had uttered the question. "I don't give a goddamn who it is you kill, you just kill 'em. 'Cepting the priest. I want him alive."

The two men exchanged a look, then turned to Mario. The scrawny one cleared his throat. "I ain't too comfortable about shooting no girl, Mario. Damn it, she's the victim in all of this."

Before Mario could reply, the Colt Artillery revolver was in Martindale's hand, the hammer cocked, the barrel aimed unerringly towards the cowpoke. "You do as I say, boy, or the only person hitting the dirt dead will be you."

"Shit, Martindale," said Mario, "you have no cause to—"

"*Do it,*" snarled Martindale through his teeth, his voice low, cold, without emotion.

With nowhere to go and nothing to do, the scrawny cowpoke kicked his horse and headed towards the rocks with his two companion close behind, their faces drained of colour.

"Listen," said Reece, "I am here to make that priest pay for what he did to Toby. That don't mean I agree with what my cousin did, but I feel I have a duty to see this through. It's my call."

Slipping the Colt back into the holster, Martindale looked without comment towards the farmhouse.

"Let it play out as it does," said Mario. "I'll go in close. You two cover me." He gestured towards a slight dip in the ground some fifty paces away to the right. "Reece, set up with your Spencer right there."

"I'm going in, too," said Martindale. "Whatever you wanna do, Reecey, that padre killed Jessup and I'm here to make him pay for it. You can have what's left of him after I've finished."

Pulling a face, Reece squirmed in the saddle and said, "I didn't think it would come to killing, if I am honest."

"Well, it has," said Martindale, "so cover us with your rifle." He kicked his horse and edged forward.

Once the gunman moved away, Mario turned to his brother. "Cover us, Reece. This whole ghastly business is coming to a head, and not before time."

"If we kill the priest, questions will be asked."

"Then we'll answer them. Or, at least, Martindale will."

"And if that US marshal arrives, what then? How will we explain the killing of the priest?"

"That's all piss in the wind, Reece. No marshal is going to come out here, and even if he did, he certainly wouldn't give a spit in hell for any low-down padre." Sucking his teeth, Mario flicked the reins and moved in behind Martindale. "Just make sure no one opens up on us – and if they do, you shoot 'em."

Dragging the back of his hand across his wet brow, Reece watched his brother trot forward. Taking a breath, he swung out of his saddle and, rifle in hand, jogged towards the dip Martindale had identified, his heart pounding in his temples, his throat dry with dust... and with fear.

Reining in his horse some fifty or so paces from the front door of the small farmhouse, Martindale glanced across to Mario who was moving up next to him. "Seems it's deserted."

"So they have gone. That means we'll have to split up and try to pick up their trail." Mario exhaled loudly. "I could do without all of this. Damn it all, we have a herd to corral and get ready for the drive next week. I can't afford the time, or the men, to do this. There are already enough of them wasting away their days, playing cards and getting drunk back in Archangel. Why did that idiot Tobias have to go and do such a stupid thing right at the worst moment?"

"He never could keep his dick in his pants."

"Yeah, but to do what he did to that girl. And she's so young. Damn it, I feel like beating him up myself."

"Well, maybe you can, after we find the priest. As soon as we—"

Without warning, the top half of the main Dutch-door to the farmhouse swung open with a loud creak, a rifle barrel appearing from the darkness within. Before either man could react, the rifle barked fire, the heavy calibre bullet slamming into Mario's chest, lifting him off the saddle.

He hit the ground on his back and lay there motionless, whilst his horse bucked and kicked and broke into a run.

From that point, all hell broke loose.

Away to the left of the tiny farmhouse, the two cowhands who had been sent to wait there exchanged bewildered, shocked looks. The scrawny one was the first to recover. He stood up, checking his revolver and then froze as an ice-cold voice drifted from somewhere behind him.

"This ain't your day, boys."

The shots rang out across the bleak, open landscape, and the two of them fell dead before they really knew what was happening, or who had killed them.

Reece crouched, rifle levelled towards the farmhouse. He saw Martindale leaping from his saddle, rolling across the dirt, already putting several shots through the still open farmhouse door. But the inert body of his brother gripped all of Reece's attention and his body convulsed in a series of juddering sobs.

"Oh no..." he managed to mumble and he stepped out from the dip and wandered forward carelessly, the tears dripping down his face, the rifle forgotten in his hands.

A shape loomed up behind him. He knew he should turn, put up some sort of resistance, but Mario was on the ground, blood seeping out from the exit wound in his back. Even when the hand grabbed him by the shoulder and pulled him around, he did nothing. The fist erupted into his guts and he folded, retching, tears and spit mixing together to splash into the dirt. The second blow connected with his jaw and he pitched over onto his side. The sky swirled around him, colours were flashing before his eyes and still he didn't care. Life was no longer worth living – they could do whatever they wanted to him, whoever they were.

He saw a foot stamp down next to his face. A foot in a worn, aged leather sandal.

"You tell your pa this is what comes of rape."

It was a voice he vaguely recognised, but the pain in his face and the despair in his heart overcame everything, and he blacked out.

Spread out in the dirt, Martindale waited. Nothing moved from within the farmhouse. Maybe he'd gotten lucky, maybe the shooter was dead. Maybe...

Maybe not.

The figure standing a few paces away occupied all his attention.

Rolling over, Martindale rose up, the Colt Artillery still in his hand. The man before him stood motionless, relaxed, hands hanging down by his sides, the gun at his right hip still holstered.

Grinning, Martindale brought up his Colt.

The figure moved, his own gun materialising as if out of thin air, his left hand fanning the hammer. Three bullets hit Martindale in an even spread across the upper torso. With his eyes wide in astonishment, his knees buckled and he crumpled to the ground, dead.

The silence was almost crushing in its totality as Ritter stepped forward and toed the dead body of the gunman. Satisfied, he quickly reloaded the used-up cartridges in his Colt Cavalry revolver, then bent down to pick up Martindale's gun.

Merry approached, massaging his fists.

"You should take this," said Ritter, offering the Colt Artillery to the padre.

"I don't need it."

"Yes, you do. We all need to be armed now. Scrimshaw's going to be coming after us with an army after what's happened here."

"I don't understand why they are so hell-bent on killing me. Nor the girls. Beat me up, run me out of town, all of that I can understand, but this..." He shook his head, then jerked himself upright as Grace charged from inside the farmhouse and ran into his arms.

Ritter watched in silence whilst the two of them held one another, then kissed.

"I felt sure they would kill you," she said breathlessly, her face smothered in his chest.

"That was a damned good shot," said Ritter.

"It wasn't me," Grace said, and nodded towards the farmhouse. Nati Parker stood in the doorway, ashen-faced, the Spencer clutched in her hands.

Grunting, Ritter looked about him. "We'll need to gather up all these firearms and whatever ammunition there is. We'll have to make another stand here."

"No," said Nati, approaching slowly, keeping her face turned away from the corpse of the man she'd shot. "We can't stay here now. We're moving on."

"You won't last more than a day out on the range," said Ritter. "The padre here is refusing to take up a gun, and although you're good with that thing, I doubt you can outshoot Scrimshaw's men."

"Then why not come with us? I have a wagon out back which we can load up with supplies, and you could ride alongside us as we—"

"Ma'am, this ain't my fight. I'm here looking for John Wesley Hardin."

"I reckon I know where he is," said Merry, in a low voice.

"He could be in a lot of places, from what I've heard."

"True, but even so, I figure I know where he is this time. Me and John go some way back. Whenever he's in trouble, he most often makes his way to one or two places, as I told you before."

"All right, you've convinced me – where has he made for?"

"I'll help you, if you can guarantee these here women your protection." He gave a wry smile. "I've not seen anyone shoot the way you have done, not ever, so my guess is they will be more than safe with you."

Ritter folded his arms and gave the priest a hard look. "Ah, shit," he said, knowing he had little choice. "All right, I guarantee it."

Smiling, Merry looked away wistfully, eyes moving across the vast expanse of sky. "There is someone – a Mexican woman. He'll go to her, to rest up and… find comfort in her arms." He turned again to face Ritter. "Her name is Maria and she is a rare beauty…" he winked, causing Ritter to gape, and added, "for a whore."

18

Ignoring the tangled corpse, the eyes of which had been plucked from its blackened head by the birds which circled squawking overhead, John Wesley Hardin strode into the little church. As he paused for a moment in the doorway, letting the coolness settle over him, he took in the bare wooden pews, the simplicity of the decorations, and the half-open door of the vestry no more than twenty feet from where he stood. Easing out his Colt, he moved down the narrow central aisle, senses alert and, on reaching the entrance to the vestry, nudged the door open with the barrel of his gun. The hinges squealed. Half expecting the priest to emerge, armed and ready, Hardin cocked the Colt, preparing to shoot.

The silence lay heavy all around, mingling with the cool air to bring an enormous sense of peace to the place, and a certain emptiness. Releasing a long breath, Hardin eased off the hammer and dropped the gun back into its holster. He went inside the tiny room and studied it for a moment. There was nothing within which spoke of a hurried escape; no overturned artefacts, no sign of a disturbance, just a simple table, a pewter platter and several wooden goblets.

He went outside again, taking his time to study the ground. Not the finest of trackers, something he himself would attest to, he could nevertheless make out the way the ground was churned up by many horses, and how the trail seemed to disappear off to the right. They knew where they were heading and it was the opposite direction to the one he felt he should follow now, a fact he found rather reassuring. With Merry long since gone, Hardin's choice was a simple one.

Many times in the past, Hardin had found himself fleeing for his life after an unfortunate altercation, pursued by a hard-nosed, unforgiving posse, intent on stringing him up from the nearest tree. The same would be happening again soon, after the killing of the cowpoke back at the Wishing Bone. So he hauled himself up into the saddle and, taking a final glance around him, he kicked his mount into a gentle canter and made his way south, a direction which would lead him eventually to the woman he liked to call his own. Maria.

19

He heard the sound of voices, the unmistakeable packing up of belongings, the neighing of horses and finally, after much movement, the steady trundling of wagon wheels. Throughout it all, Reece dared not move. Perhaps, if his gun was to hand, he may have attempted a few measured shots, but he doubted it. He'd witnessed Martindale being shot dead with frightening ease by the unknown gunman. Apart from this, he knew the priest had taken his guns, both revolver and rifle. Bullets, too. There was nothing to do except listen, wait, and remain still.

As the wagon creaked and groaned off into the distance, he chanced a look through one eye and saw them – two women on the buckboard, steering the open wagon, and three riders alongside. The tall stranger, the massive bulk of Merry, and another woman. Their movements were slow and unhurried and he pondered on where they might be heading.

Swallowing down his natural inclination to get up and run to his dead brother's side, Reece remained motionless, controlling his breathing. Even when a lone buzzard flapped just above him and settled not three paces away to study him with its jaundiced eyes, he lay inert. Only when completely satisfied that the tiny band were well out of sight, did he slowly roll over, put his palms into the ground, and arch himself up to his knees.

Releasing an angry cry, the great, ugly bird sprang back in alarm and took off, landing again some several yards away, where it remained, watching. Wincing, Reece tenderly touched his throbbing jaw, reached down for a stone and hurled it at the bird, which flew off. He watched the affronted creature disappearing into the distance, no doubt going off to seek out others of its flock and bring them back to the awaiting feast.

Mario, Martindale and the other two. All dead.

He raked in a breath and looked across to his brother, his eyes transfixed at the sight of the horrible hole in his chest, black with dried blood. Biting his lip hard, he swallowed down his anguish and climbed to his feet.

As he checked around, his initial suspicions that his firearms had been taken proved correct. They had even stripped Martindale and Mario of their gun belts, collecting enough ammunition to see them through their journey, wherever that might be.

No longer caring who they were or where they headed, Reece staggered across to his brother and dropped to his knees. Tears rolled unchecked through the grime of his cheeks. "Oh, sweet Jesus, Mario, I'm so sorry." He dipped forward, took up his brother's head in his hands and cradled him to his chest, sobbing uncontrollably.

He remained like that for a long time.

With due solemnity and care, Reece managed to place his brother's corpse across the back of Martindale's horse. The other animals had long since galloped off, terrified by the violence which had so suddenly and swiftly erupted all around them. Thanking God for this small piece of good fortune, Reece took the reins and led the horse and its tragic burden in the direction of his father's ranch. He had never dreaded anything as much as what lay ahead... having to tell his father about what had occurred, and that all of it was caused by the recklessness of Toby, and Reece's desire to avenge his wastrel half-brother for the beating he had taken at the hands of the priest.

If only he had left everything alone, none of this would have happened. Jessup, Martindale and Mario would all still be alive. The priest, damn him, could have sat in his church and prayed to God for forgiveness, and Tobias would have been soundly thrashed by his father. Life would have continued. But not now. Now, there was nothing to look forward to in a world changed out of all recognition.

And God alone knew what old man Scrimshaw's reaction would be.

Trying to keep the awfulness of what lay ahead from occupying his mind, Reece slowly led the horse with its heavy load away from that dreadful place of death, his eyes lowered, his tears dripping to the ground below.

Behind him, the buzzards came and settled, nervous of any more unexpected movements from the remaining bodies.

But there were none.

Only the promise of feasting remained.

20

Perhaps it was his third neat whisky, perhaps it was his fourth. He didn't know, didn't care. Silas Scrimshaw sat and stared into the bottom of his glass, mourning the passing of his son, Reece. For it was a passing. The lines had been drawn, the speeches made. He'd banished Reece into the darkness, disowning him, and it was all so unnecessary.

He swilled the last mouthful around the bottom of the glass and threw the contents down his throat and sat, face in hands, and sobbed.

"You shouldn't punish yourself so."

Lowering his hands, he looked up to see her standing there, as beautiful as an angel. Manuela. She'd brought life back, not only to his loins, but to his whole, withering existence. And here she was, with that smouldering look of hers, those lips that were so full, but not smiling this time. Concerned, instead. Hard.

"I can't take any of it anymore," he said. "The bickering, the nonsense. I just want a quiet life, time to live out my last few years with you."

She quickly moved in front of him, falling to her knees, holding his hands in hers. "Don't talk like that. We have many years ahead of us. This thing with Reece, it will blow over."

"No," he said sadly. Dragging his hands from her grasp, he stared at his palms for a moment, then squeezed them into fists. "No."

Her own hands were strong, those long, brown fingers like bands of steel. She gripped his wrists and stared at him. "Don't give up. He is your son."

"I said such terrible things."

"He will understand. He will beg your forgiveness."

"I need to beg him for his."

"That is not how I heard it. He is... how do you say it... hard-headed? He does not think of the consequences of his words. Toby, he did a terrible thing. He must be punished for that."

"That girl is thirteen."

"I know. That is unforgiveable."

Taking a shuddering breath, Silas reached out and stroked her cheek. She tilted her head into the warmth of his palm and sighed. "You're so beautiful," he said and leaned forward, kissing her lightly on the lips.

They both jumped as old Grimes, Silas's faithful servant, blasted into the room, out of breath, face like death. He was wringing his hands and there were tears in his eyes.

"What is it?" Silas asked. He was already dreading the answer.

"It's Master Reece, boss. He's out front."

A quick exchange of looks flashed between Silas and Manuela. Her eyes were alight with hope, but all he could feel was dread. "Master Reece?"

"You'd better come outside, boss. He's got Master Mario with him."

Frowning, Silas stood up. "The two of them? What's going on?"

Grimes stepped aside, gesturing to the open door which led into the main entrance room and beyond, to the front yard. "You'd better take a look, boss."

Silas was one of the old breed of cattle-barons, carved out of the dirt and dust of the prairie. He'd grown up with the taste of the range clinging to the back of his throat like a part of him, a constant reminder of who he was and where he came from. Those tender years, from around the age of fifteen to twenty, had seen him living his days in the saddle and his nights rolled up in a threadbare blanket, suffering the vagaries of the weather.

He'd seen much while he was out there, exposed to the elements. He'd witnessed men, strapping men, fine men, gored to death by the horns of a crazed bullock, testing its strength on the soft, unforgiving flesh of those who tried to tame it. Gunfights, in which men had killed and died with little conscience for either. Whores, play-acting their finest screams and groans, drinking, gambling. And Indians. Comanche for the most part, coming out of the blood-red dust like phantoms from hell, their wild eyes and bronzed bodies rigid with desire to kill, maim and scalp. Many a night he'd lay prone behind a clump of rocks, his Winchester at the ready, only to find the morning sun bringing the evidence of another silent night's raid. Men with their throats slit, their brains spilled out in the dirt.

But none of this prepared him for what he saw now.

His son, Mario, draped over the back of a horse, his hair stiff and matted, skin sallow, that awful, sickening hole in his back so big... so black.

He moved towards this scene as if in a dream, steps heavy, his eyes registering but not believing. His boy. His life. *Dear God, why has it come to this?*

After a slight pause, during which the only sound was his ragged breaths rasping in his tight chest, he pressed his face into the sweat-stained shirt of his boy, Reece, and wept.

No one spoke, no one dared. This was Silas Scrimshaw's moment, no one else's. Even Manuela stood in reverent silence, wringing her hands, tears tumbling down her lovely face, those huge, black eyes of hers filled with despair. And Grimes slumped against the wall, whimpering, his body crumpling, an old frame too weak to withstand the enormity of this grief.

For his part, Reece stood rock-still and downcast, wishing he knew what to say, wishing it was yesterday, last week, last year. Any day but here and now.

"Who did this?"

The words sounded muffled, as Silas' face was still embedded in his son's shirt.

Reece raked in a breath. "We went to the ranch. Five of us. Mario, Martindale and—"

"I asked you who did it."

Reece turned a pleading face towards Manuela and his voice, when it came, sounded like the bleating of a lost lamb. "Hell, Pa, *I don't know.*"

"You don't know?" Silas, gripping Reece's shirt hard in his hands, raised his head, exposing a face alive with sorrow mingled with a deep and all-consuming rage. "You were *there*, God damn you! *Who the hell killed him?*"

"It happened so quick, I didn't really—" He stopped, the look in his father's eyes freezing the very marrow in his bones. He tried to take a step backwards, but old man Silas was strong, his grip unfaltering.

Reece brought up his hands. "Pa, *for God's sake*! Someone fired a shot from out of the cabin and Mario went down. Then everything just went crazy."

"And you?" Dropping his grip, Silas glared into his son's face. "What happened to you?"

Reece stroked his jaw, wincing at the swelling. "That damn priest, he beat me down."

"He beat you down?"

"Yes. Took my gun and left me for dead."

"He beat you down and took your gun?"

"That's what I said. Jesus, it happened so quick. Martindale, he... aw, shit, some gunman, the like I've never seen, blew him apart. Three bullets in the chest, quicker than a rattler."

"And all the while the priest was beating you?"

Swallowing hard, Reece shot Manuela another look, a look which begged her to help, to step in and make Silas understand.

But Manuela did nothing.

Then Silas moved. For an old man, he moved fast, and his strength was frightening. He gripped Reece around the throat, throttling him one-handedly. Squawking and kicking, Reece held onto his father's hand with both of his, but no amount of effort could tear away that grip of steel. His knees buckling, Reece crumpled, but Silas did not ease up. He merely peered down at his son with murderous eyes blazing with hatred.

And nobody else moved or said a word, even when Reece collapsed unconscious to the ground.

Slowly, Silas spread out his quivering hands and broke down in tears. But nobody spoke. Not for a long, long time.

21

"Very wonderful things, aren't they?"

Ritter took the binoculars from Natis hands and studied them as if for the first time. "Yes, I suppose they are."

They'd pulled into a small pass between groups of towering rocks and Ritter had decided to climb up to the top of one of them to gain a good view of the sprawling plain around them. As he flattened himself down amongst the scree and pulled out his German-made field glasses, Nati scrambled up beside him, breathless but eager. He looked at her and, not for the first time, lost himself in her wide, black eyes. Her rich, nutmeg-coloured skin shone with health, her prominent cheek-bones acting almost like a mirror, reflecting the bright sunlight. She caught him looking and smiled. Embarrassed, he turned away, fitted the binoculars to his eyes and almost immediately sucked in his breath.

"What is it?"

He passed her the glasses and, after pressing them against her eyes and sweeping them from left to right across the vista, she saw it, too.

Dust.

Riders.

Now, as they both lay there, Merry's voice came to them from below. "Can you see anything?"

"Should I tell him?"

Ritter shrugged. "I'll need that rifle of yours."

"You gonna shoot 'em?"

"I have to stop them, if that's what you mean."

"It's not."

Arching a single eyebrow, his eyes fell to her lips. A tiny, random thought stirred his memory, something he'd read or heard about, that staring at a person's mouth when they spoke was supposed to mean something, but just what, he couldn't remember.

"Have you ever fired a rifle this far?"

Her voice sounded husky, coated perhaps by the inhalation of dust from the ride. She'd perched herself on the buckboard of the wagon, with no scarf or bonnet, only her thick black hair, tied back in a pony-tail, protecting her from the sun. He watched her lips as she spoke, then laughed and turned back to view the vast expanse of country, and the puffs of dust betraying the approach of riders. "I'll wait. Maybe they aren't following us."

"You know that's not true."

He nodded. "Yep. I know it."

"So... can you?" She jutted her chin towards their pursuers. "Shoot from this range?"

"Time will tell," he said and rolled onto his back. He sat up. "I'll fetch the rifle."

"*Can you see anything?*" called Merry once again.

"I'll fetch it," said Nati.

"The shot you took on that first cowboy..." His voice trailed away.

"That was Mario. One of the Scrimshaw boys."

"That was a helluva shot." He'd meant it to sound like praise. Truth was, he'd rarely seen a single shot so well taken. And she'd never mentioned it since. To kill a man. That is not a normal occurrence for a young, handsome-looking woman living with only her younger sister for company. Maybe it was the rape which had made her so cold, so unflinching. Maybe.

Without answering, she gathered up her skirts and scrambled across the flat cliff top and soon disappeared over the lip, out of his sight. He sat for a moment, considering how he might turn the next round of conversation to more meaningful things. He liked her. Liked her a lot.

And yet there was something, a barrier of some kind, which prevented him from, or at least made him hesitate in, asking her about herself... what she liked, what she hoped for in life. Perhaps, when all of this nonsense was over and Hardin was in his grave, he might even ask her out. Hell, he might even try to steal a kiss.

Nati strode towards the others, went straight to Ritter's horse and withdrew the Sharps from its sheath. She checked the load, then reached into one of the nearby saddle bags and began to drop extra cartridges into one of the pockets in her work dress.

"What's happening out there?" asked Merry, unable to disguise the anxiety on his face.

"There's a group of riders coming up fast."

"Oh, my God," said Grace, unconsciously slipping her arm through Merry's. "How many of them?"

"Difficult to say." She lifted the rifle slightly. "Ritter means to hold 'em up."

"By killing them?" Merry's voice sounded tremulous and thick with disbelief.

"I reckon."

"Hasn't there been enough killing?" he asked, shaking his head. Grace pressed herself even closer against him and he put his arm around her.

"It's not going to stop, Father," Nati said. "Not until them Scrimshaws are in the ground. You know it, so do I."

"This is all my fault," said the priest, pressing the fingers of his free hand against his eyes. As he squeezed, the tears seeped through.

"No. This is all to do with that bastard who did what he did to Flo. He's the one to blame, Father."

"I lost my temper. I should never—"

Leaning forward, Nati squeezed his arm. "I'm glad you did."

Dropping his hand, he looked at her through eyes red-rimmed and wet with tears. "Forgiveness is what I've preached all of my life as a priest. I let my former self gain advantage and this is the result."

"No," she said. "No. You're not the one who's done wrong. Those Scrimshaws think they can do what the hell they like, to whoever they like. Well, that ain't so and it stops here and it stops now."

"Nati," said Grace, her voice barely a whisper, "what has happened to you?"

Her eyes went cold. "I've woken up, is all. The pity is, it took something like this to make me open my eyes and see what needed to be done."

"Killing?" said Merry.

She snapped her head to the priest. "If need be. There's no going back after what that bastard did. You think he would have taken your beating and changed his ways?"

"I don't know. Maybe. If I hadn't—"

"If you hadn't, he'd have come back for more. And more. And he'd have kept coming until I'd shot him, and then what? Reece and Mario would have come, just like they did, but Ritter wouldn't be here, and neither would you. We'd be dead, Father. After they'd all raped us." She put the heel of one hand into her eye and sniffed loudly. "No, this is the best outcome for all of us. Believe me, Father, sometimes you have to do the unthinkable in order to live."

Another sniff and she swung around and made her way back to the rock-face, scurrying up the steep slope without a backward glance.

Ritter twisted his head as Nati came up alongside him. "You took your time."

"Father Merry was giving one of his sermons." She worked the rifle, feeding a cartridge into the breech. "I had to put him right on a few things." She grinned. "How many?"

"Four."

She took the field glasses and picked them out. They were now clearly visible, old man Scrimshaw at the front, an even older man next to him, and two other riders in chaps and wide-brimmed Stetsons. "Can you take the shot, Ritter?"

"I can try."

"That ain't good enough. You miss, they'll dash for cover and then make their way around us, as well as in front. They'll bottle us up in the pass with no way out."

"You seem to know a lot about this."

"Pa was in the army. He told me some things. I guess I was the son he'd never had."

"You're the prettiest looking *son* I've ever seen." The words caught him unawares, bursting out as if on their own volition and he looked away, the heat rising to his cheeks.

She gave a tiny chuckle. "In another time, Ritter... who knows?"

For something to do, he tore off his gloves and reached out his hands. "Let me take a shot."

"It's too risky."

"Then what the hell do you propose."

She tilted her head, her eyes flat, without emotion. "I'll do it."

22

At the first splash of cold water across his face, Reece sat bolt upright, his hands wildly dashing away invisible attackers as he struggled to escape.

"Reece," she said, pressing him back down with her strong hands locked around his shoulder, "Reece, it's all right – it's over."

Blinking, he looked up into Manuela's face and it was as if the whole world had been replaced by the loveliness of her features. In a rush of relief and gratitude at being alive, he flung his arms around her and pulled her close. She held him and they kissed, the fire of their passion pushing every other emotion, fear and thought far, far away.

After a long time, she gently pressed him down on the bed and examined his throat, dabbing the raised welts, using a damp cloth that she dipped into the bucket standing next to the bed.

He watched her, biting down the sharp stabs of pain as the water hit the tender areas of broken, swollen flesh. "Why didn't you stop him?"

The sharp, brittle tone of his voice caused her to stop and she gazed into his eyes, unblinking. "What would you have had me do? Shoot him?"

"Maybe. You could have done something."

"He was like a man on fire – consumed with anger, even hate."

"Yes. Hate. For his son."

"A son he'd disowned."

"Oh, so that's it? That's your reason? Because he no longer considered me his son?"

Blowing out her breath in a rush, she threw the cloth forcibly into the bucket, sending the water slopping over the rim. "If I'd have done anything, he would have suspected something."

"Oh, and you don't think he does already? Your afternoon rides across the prairie? You don't think he knows where you're going?"

"How could he? And if he did, he would surely kill you."

"Which is what he tried to do earlier."

Her demeanour changed from exasperation, to consideration, then finally to deflation. With heavy, slumped shoulders, she turned away and moved over to the half-shuttered window. Pulling back one of the twin shutters, she peered out across the Scrimshaw ranch, lost in thought.

"I'll gather the cattle I've been ferreting away," Reece said, "then we'll get the hell away from here. It's what we always planned to do. Now's our chance."

Without turning, she continued gazing into the distance. "Once he's killed the priest and he realises what we've done, he'll come after us. He won't stop until he finds us."

"We'll head for Mexico. He won't follow us there."

She swung around, glaring. "Listen to yourself! He'll follow us to the gates of hell if need be, and you know it."

"One thing is for sure – we can't stay here."

"We cannot run, either."

Expelling a sharp breath, Reece eased himself to a sitting position. Carefully, he touched the tender skin of his bruised throat with his fingertips and studied them thoughtfully. Finally, in a low and serious voice, he said, "Then there is only one solution." Wincing slightly, he turned his head to look directly at her. "I'll kill him when he returns."

Silence developed like a gulf between them and, as the first few teardrops sprouted, she looked again at the expanse of the ranch, and murmured at last, "You think you can?"

"I don't have a choice."

"Every lawman in the county will be on our trail. He has everybody in his pocket, you know that."

"Yes, but they can't go to Mexico."

Nodding, she closed her eyes and wondered why life, even in its lighter moments, was forever tinged with pain and sadness.

23

Something flashed through the thick, hot late afternoon air, a red-hot trail streaking towards the small group of riders and Scrimshaw cried out, his body bucking as the heavy impact struck him with tremendous power. Even before he slipped from his saddle, the sound of the gunshot rang out across the vast, empty landscape.

Grimes reacted first, mouth open in a wide, terrified gape. Screaming out his beloved master's name, he jumped down, tried and failed to catch Scrimshaw before he hit the dirt, then broke into a series of bleats and howls that rang out like the cries of a stricken beast across the plain.

Scrimshaw lay on his back, blinking up into the sky, as bewilderment, followed by shock, seized him in a vice-like grip. "Oh Christ," he breathed.

"Hold on, Mr Scrimshaw, sir," said Grimes. He squatted down next to his master, staring in disbelief at the patch of crimson slowly spreading across Scrimshaw's chest. Around him, the other two men were bent double, heading for cover, their guns drawn.

"Fetch me water!" screamed the old retainer, but neither of the cow-pokes was in any mood to offer assistance, self-survival being their only concern. "Bastards," breathed Grimes. Ripping away his neckerchief, he loosened Scrimshaw's collar and pressed the piece of material onto the wound. Scrimshaw hissed, back arching. Picking up his master's hand, he guided it to the hole in the man's shirt. "Hold tight, Mr Scrimshaw, sir."

"What in the hell happened?"

"You been shot. Hold on, I'll get some water."

"Shot?" Scrimshaw shook his head, lips trembling, searching the broad expanse of white sky above him. "*Shot?*"

Grimes stood up and the bullet hit him in the small of his back. He yelped, hands clutching instinctively at the entry point as the sound of the heavy calibre bullet followed less than a second afterwards.

Falling to his knees, Grimes gazed towards the horses. All four were skittish, kicking at the ground, terror spreading from one to the other, infecting them with all the swiftness of an ancient, irresistible disease.

"*Ahhh, God,*" rasped Grimes, reaching out towards the terrified animals. Even as he moved, he knew it was useless. Their nostrils were wide, their eyes were rolling and they all looked as if they were about to break into a wild stampede. "Willis," he croaked, "Willis, don't let them bolt."

But Willis was not about to break cover and when Grimes turned to stare directly at the cowpoke, he saw the fear in his eyes and accepted the hopelessness of it all and knew nothing good was going to come out of this situation.

Behind him, Scrimshaw groaned and Grimes wanted so much to help, the way he had done all his life, the faithful, constant servant, his love for his master total. Was it too much to beg for just a few more moments? One last effort to bring water to the lips of the man he idolised?

It was too much to ask and, even as he attempted to gather his strength, his life drained from him in a rush and he pitched lifeless into the dirt.

Pausing to wipe the sweat from her brow, Nati blew out her breath and pushed the next cartridge into the breach. Beside her, Ritter pursed his lips and lowered the field glasses. "Those were two impressive shots."

"Only one of them is dead."

"What about the two cowpokes?"

"They can rot for all I care." Licking her lips, she swung up the rifle and squinted down the barrel. "I'm going to send a shot next to the horses and spook 'em enough to force 'em to break."

"Without horses, they'll die out here."

"Exactly."

Her upper body jerked slightly as she loosed off the shot. A tell-tale puff of dust sprang up close to the lead horse's hooves and it immediately reared up, its scream of fear carrying all the way across the open plain. Within a blink, the entire group of animals broke out in a mad dash towards imagined safety, bucking and kicking as they went, sending up great clouds of sand to partially disguise their flight.

There was no disguising the reactions of the two cowpokes, however. Careless of their own safety, both broke cover, flapping their arms and waving their hats in a desperate attempt to slow, if not stop, the horses.

They failed and Ritter chuckled as he watched them through the binoculars.

Nati slid in the next cartridge, working with slow, methodical precision. "I can't get a good shot at Scrimshaw as he's lying partially hidden, but I can put a bullet into his inner thigh. He'll bleed out within the hour and we can forget all about him."

With the glasses still pressed against his face, Ritter blew out a silent whistle. "You must be right on the edge of that rifle's range. You think you can do it?"

"I have done so far, wouldn't you say?"

"More than, but this is going to take some doing. You've got about six inches of leg to shoot at."

She grunted, took careful aim and fired.

It took little more than a second for the heavy calibre bullet to cross the thousand yards to its target.

Lowering the rifle slowly, Nati glanced across at him and Ritter, putting aside the glasses, gave her a long look. "That's it then," he said, and sighed. "You're an incredible woman, Nati."

She didn't react at all. "We can continue on our way without fear now," she said and got to her feet.

He followed her, but, before she could take another step, he reached out and took hold of her arm, swung her to him and kissed her forcibly.

She did not resist. Her lips melded into his, the rifle slipping to the ground at her feet, no longer needed, its job done.

24

"We'll swing south in the morning," said Merry, as he watched the others coming down from the top of the rock. Both appeared breathless – not just from the climb, surmised Merry. "I'm assuming he's dead?"

"They'll all be dead pretty soon enough," said Ritter, crossing to his horse and unhitching his water canteen. He pulled out the stopper and offered it to Nati first, who took it and drank deeply before returning it to the gunfighter.

"Hardin's woman lives just inside the Mexican border," said Merry. "I reckon we will be about two days behind him, now that we don't have to hurry. By the time any lawmen learn of Scrimshaw's death, we'll be well on the way."

"It's you they'll pin the old man's death on," said Nati.

They all looked at her, but no one spoke. The truth of her words was incontestable. Merry nodded, shooting Grace a quick look. "I know it." His mouth creased into a wan smile. "I can live with that."

"Are you sure?"

"I wouldn't have been able to remain here, anyway," said the priest. Grace came to him and he hugged her, wrapping her arms around his waist.

"What will you do, padre?" asked Ritter. "None of this is your fight. You don't owe me anything, and now we're all in the shit together."

"I was already in it, well before you showed up."

"But you knew Hardin, you have no beef with him." Ritter sucked in a breath, his hands on his hips, kicking at the ground with the toe of his boot. "I guess what I'm trying to say is, with Scrimshaw out of the way, it might be best for you two strike out on your own."

"The journey south will be long and fraught with danger," said Merry. "We need you with us. I have no feelings for Hardin. We crossed paths, that is all. What you are set on doing is your own affair. We'll find something when we get there. Eke out a living, start again."

"I have money," said Grace. They all looked at her in surprise. She smiled. "My former profession paid well, and I've been careful."

Over at the wagon, Florence broke out in a loud guffaw. It seemed to relieve the heavy mood and they all went about their business, preparing their various horses. Nati crossed over and climbed up next to her sister.

As Grace went to join them, Merry walked up to Ritter just as the gunfighter was about to swing up into his saddle. "Are you sure he's dead?"

"He will be. She shot him through the thigh, and we both know what that means."

The priest stopped and gaped. "*She*? I assumed it was you who—"

"She did it all."

"My God!" Merry gasped, looking across towards Nati. "What happened to Florence has changed her."

"It's changed us all, padre."

"Not you." Merry held the gunman's eyes. "You're used to killing, but the girls…"

"You'd think she'd been doing it all her life, the way she took them out. She said something about her father, and the War. How he taught her to shoot."

"They were dangerous times."

"They still are. The War is still working its horrors, padre. You met Hardin back then?"

"No, he was only a boy. I came across him some years later, when I was a novice, a couple of months before I took my vows. Vows which I have now well and truly broken."

"What you did was perfectly understandable."

"Yes, but everything that has happened in its wake… I'll never forgive myself." He shrugged and sighed. "I should have left well alone."

"So that bastard could do it all again? No one was ever going to bring him to book."

"Even so…"

"Well," said Ritter and settled himself into the saddle, "it is what it is and there's an end to it." He reached forward and stroked the neck of his horse. "What's done is done, padre. There ain't nothing any of us can do about it now. We'll head down to Mexico, you can point me in Hardin's direction, and that'll be that."

"He's dangerous."

Nodding, Ritter adjusted his hat, lowering the brim until his eyes were in deep shadow. "So am I, padre. So am I," and he flicked his reins and moved ahead of the wagon, which Nati slowly steered in behind him.

25

On the morning of the second day, Tobias Scrimshaw rolled over onto his side, blinked open his eyes and licked his dry lips. "I need a drink," he groaned. He swung his legs from under the bedclothes and sat up. Screwing up his face, he looked down at the bandages wrapped around his ribcage, then gingerly touched his nose with his fingers. It felt strange and misshapen under his touch.

"Shit, I feel like I've been hit by a freight train." He went to stand up, and hissed as a stab of pain forced him back down again.

"You shouldn't be moving around too much," said the big, burly man coming through the main door at a rush. His short sleeves were rolled up past his impressive biceps, and his hands dripped water, as if he had only just finished washing. He put one pan-sized palm against Tobias's chest and eased him back into the bed.

"I'm all right," said Tobias, but he didn't feel it. A whooshing sound reverberated between his ears and his ribs hurt more than he could have feared to believe.

"You don't look it."

Prising open one eye, Tobias considered the bulk of the man standing over him. "Where in hell am I?"

"You're in my surgery. I'm a doctor. I patched you up as best I could, but if you go rushing around like some wild steer, you're gonna end up in a sanatorium."

"A doctor? A surgery? What the hell?"

"You don't remember anything?"

Shaking his head, Tobias did his best to cast his mind back. "Vaguely. I remember being in the bar before I got drunk. Mario and me, some of the boys, drinking like there was no tomorrow."

"You remember who beat you up?"

A vague, ghost-like image reared up behind his eyes, lacking all sense of form and physiology. "Nope. I remember feeling like I'd been hit by a sledge-hammer." He subconsciously trailed his finger-tips across his still swollen jaw. "But what in hell it was really, I have no idea."

"You recollect the girl?"

"Girl? What girl?"

The big man drew in a deep breath. "The one you violated?"

"Violated? What the hell do you mean by that?"

"What I say. That was the reason you got the crap beaten out of you. You upset a lot of people with what you did."

Tobias closed his eyes, thinking back. Some of the apparitions took shape, solidifying in front of his mind's eye. "Nope. Not a damn thing." He gazed up at the doctor. "I want to thank you, Doc. I'm guessing I was in a bad way."

"You was. I was honour-bound to tend to you, even though I would have preferred to see you bleed out in the gutter."

"Jeez, Doc," Tobias twisted his face away. "I'd best get back to my pa's ranch. He'll be worrying about me."

"I doubt that."

"Eh?" Gritting his teeth, Tobias sat up, taking several short breaths to steady himself. "I reckon he will. I need to get dressed."

"You need to rest."

"No, damn it, I've rested enough. I need to get back to the ranch, speak to Mario. This whole business is a heap of shit and I need to fix it. Pass me my pants."

The doctor did so, tossing over the still dirty work clothes, together with Tobias's gun belt. Grunting with the effort, Tobias struggled out of the bed and painfully pulled on his clothes. All the time, the doctor watched him, his face blank, his mouth a thin line, but his obvious disgust at the injured man in front of him seeping out of every pore.

Adjusting his belt, Tobias checked the Navy Colt conversion model, counting the five loaded cartridges. He, along with many individuals, considered it a safety precaution to leave the hammer resting on an empty chamber. "How much do I owe you, Doc?"

"Just get out of my surgery," said the doctor. "That'll be payment enough."

"If you say so."

"I do. Your horse is stabled out back. Some young firebrand brought you in on the back of it. I can't recall his name. He said he was coming back but he never showed."

"Oh." Tobias pursed his lips, studying his gun as if for the first time. "What did you mean when you said you didn't think my pa would be worrying about me?"

The doctor pulled in another deep breath. "Well, I may as well tell you, as the whole town is full of the news." He lowered his head slightly to stare at Tobias from under his heavy, seemingly troubled brows. "Your pa is dead. Shot."

If confusion and irritation had conspired to cause him severe stress, they were as nothing compared to what Tobias felt now. Lurching backwards, he groped for the bed and flopped down onto it, mouth hanging open, disbelief threatening to overwhelm him. "What in the hell…?"

"They found him out on the range. Him and some old dried-up guy, and two cowboys, one of whom was dead. The other recounted the story, once he'd recovered. The priest, the one called Merry, he'd done for them all."

"The priest…?"

"The very same man who beat you within an inch of your life. A man of God, although what God he can possible follow is beyond me."

Rocked by a sharp jerk of grief, Tobias pitched forward, his gun dropping to the ground forgotten, his beefy hands slapping up into his face. As he rocked backwards and forwards, he emitted sobs so powerful that anyone within earshot might think they would break him apart.

The minutes ticked by.

Tobias, his thoughts clouded by the impossibility of the doctor's words, allowed his shock and misery to run their course, at least for the moment. His father was always a hard, bitter old man, but there were times in the past when he had showed kindness, even humour. Times when the world seemed a good place, a gentle, peaceful place in which all manner of dreams and ambitions were possible.

"When Ma died," he said, muttering through his fingers, "I was nothing more than a squirt. Maybe four. He buried her and I remember at the graveside, we all prayed, and even then he had Mario's mother next to him." He dragged his hands from his face. "But I never stopped loving that old bastard. He gave me next to nothin', leaving all responsibility to Mario. Me and Reece, we were the ones left out, but we never got on, me and him. Mario, he was like the father I should have had."

"Well, he's dead, too."

The doctor's words sounded as if they were being dragged through a river of molasses, so long and drawn out and thick they were.

"What in the hell...? What are you telling me, you son of a bitch?"

"I'm telling you how it is. Best you know now, rather than go scooting off to a saloon to hear it from the mouth of some drunken ingrate."

"*What?*"

They looked at one another, a gulf between them, a gulf of unknowing. Then, in a wild flurry of movement, Tobias reached down and swept up the Colt. He fired three shots into the doctor, blind shots, un-aimed, all his pent-up grief and rage focused in on that single act of violence. The gunshots boomed out around the tiny surgery, each bullet slamming into the bulk of the doctor's torso, spinning him on his heels, sending him crashing into a medicine cabinet standing against the far wall. He grasped at it in a futile effort to keep himself on his feet, but Tobias put the last two bullets into the man's back and he slid to the side, blood leaking from his wounds. Folding into a heap, he lay still, the smell of cordite thick in the air, the only sound that of Tobias's heavy breathing.

He stood over the body for a long time, a thin curl of blue smoke trailing from the barrel of his gun, and he knew right there and right then that he would hunt down the priest and end his miserable existence, if it took him the rest of his life to do so.

About the Author

Stuart G Yates is the author of a eclectic mix of books, ranging from historical fiction through to contemporary thrillers. Hailing from Merseyside, he now lives in southern Spain, where he teaches history, but dreams of living on a narrowboat in Shropshire.

Made in the USA
Middletown, DE
27 July 2020